Colin R Parsons is a children's fiction author who writes in many genres. He has a plethora of books and short stories published. His fantasy, sci-fi, supernatural and steam-punk books are popular with children and adults alike. He lives with his wife, Jan, in Wales in the UK, and is proud to be Welsh. If he's not visiting schools or writing, you can find him trying to figure out the problems of time and space.

www.colinrparsons.com

WIZARDS' EXILE

To 5A
Best Wishes

Colin R. Parsons

WIZARDS' EXILE

Pegasus

A CIP catalogue record for this title is
available from the British Library.

ISBN 9781910903186

*Pegasus is an imprint of
Pegasus Elliot MacKenzie Publishers Ltd.*
www.pegasuspublishers.com

First Published in 2019

**Pegasus
Sheraton House Castle Park
Cambridge England**

Printed & Bound in Great Britain

ALSO BY COLIN R PARSONS

HOUSE OF DARKE

D. I. S. C. Direct Interface Shadow Control

GHOSTED

Dedication

For Kristoffer and Ryan –
My two sons who have supported me in
my writing career – from my very first
scribbles.

Acknowledgments

My wife Jan and family, goes without saying.
My thanks though, must rest with my readers.
Without their dedication and sincerity my
writing wouldn't mean a thing.

Introduction

Obsidian the wizard was the ruler of the sky city of Valusha, and everyone seemed happy. The city itself was populated with roads, buildings and open fields with trees and even a river that flowed through it.

Originally, in order to live in the sky city though, someone in your family had to have a skill, a purpose. This skill would benefit the running of the city and therefore allow its population to thrive.

Jenta-Lor was campaigning in the background and eventually got elected ruler, which pushed Obsidian out. He then banned all magic from the city. This meant that all wizards had to stop practising it or be exiled, even imprisoned. Most of the small band of wizards escaped and left Valusha under cover of night, in whatever capacity they could. Obsidian disappeared too, and was never heard of again. Any remaining wizards who retaliated were sent to Skytraz Prison.

*****

Rhidian Fines was accepted as a citizen in Valusha because of his engineering skills. He was a whiz with machinery. He met, fell in love, and married Mia White.

Rhidian then worked for Jenta-Lor, fixing and repairing things. Soon he became known as "the engineer". Once Jenta-Lor had discovered there was a highly skilled engineer in the city, he had him study and invent an anti-magnetic technology that was used for powering cars and many other things. Jenta-Lor then appointed Morbid (his spy) to work with, and learn from, Rhidian.

Out of nowhere, a Jenta-Lor Police Force was put into place, enforcing any laws Jenta-Lor established. But the people soon discovered that the new ruler wasn't there to help them, and then things began to change...

Chapter 1
Night Arrest

The two officers trudged along the ground in a quickstep march. The only significant difference in their appearance was that one was slightly taller than the other. They wore the signature black uniform, which was topped off with silver-tipped helmets and a full-face visor, which only left a slit for their eyes. The hardened shell of their body armour squeaked and creaked as they moved stealthily through the night. These were part of the Jenta Police Force, an army of police officers, who served Jenta-Lor. They enforced the law in the sky city of Valusha.

The streets were quiet at that time of night and all that could be heard was a dog barking in the distance. The two soldiers had their orders and were ready and able to implement them. Their target was close.

*****

Rhidian grimaced while he clenched his teeth and tightened the last turn of the bolt. A thin line of sweat trickled down his brow, eventually culminating in droplets off his nose. He wiped away the excess perspiration with the sleeve of his shirt before it stung his eyes – he hated that. He knew once he started the machine the outer casing had to be safe, so the metal guard had to be fully tight – he didn't want any accidents.

He grunted as he wrestled with the spanner, gave it one last effort and then grinned in satisfaction. He glanced at the glass dial showing the pressure gauge and gave it a tap.

'Looks fine,' he said with a cheery sigh. 'Time to get this thing started, eh, Morbid?' There was a hint of admiration in his eyes. He loved working on new mechanical projects, and the pleasure it gave him when it worked was immeasurable.

Rhidian Fines was an engineer in his early thirties. He was a tall, lean man with a pale complexion. The cause of the bleached-white skin was far too many days in the workshop, instead of outside taking in the fresh air. He swept his sandy curls from his brow, for what seemed the umpteenth time. The sweat had dampened his locks and plastered the ends of his hair to his forehead. Rhidian's green eyes surveyed the finer points of the machine one more time. He'd played the scenario over in his head a thousand times, and as far as he was concerned everything was in place.

'Right, let's try this then,' he chirped with anticipation, and peered at his assistant, who very rarely replied or acknowledged him. Morbid stood silently by as usual, and stared back. He was Rhidian's apprentice and had been for the past five years. Morbid, too, was pale, much more so than Rhidian. He had a small face, etched with worry lines. He always wore black, and there was something sinister about him that Rhidian just couldn't put his finger on. He only spoke to ask certain questions and then fell silent again. Morbid didn't react to Rhidian's comments and stood pensive, like a vulture surveying its prey.

'OK then,' Rhidian said, the excitement building. He was about to throw the switch. 'Here goes nothing…' He reached out, but before he could do so, there was a humongous crash that reverberated around the workshop. Rhidian flinched at the intrusion, but Morbid didn't move a single muscle. The door to the workshop had burst open and a shower of splinters and dust bloomed from the impact. There wasn't really time to react before two of Jenta-Lor's police officers walked through the grey haze. Rhidian was still trying to figure out what was happening. Then, he suddenly found his voice.

'Wha-what's going on?' he stammered. 'What is the meaning of this?' He looked directly into the eyes of one of the officers. 'You didn't have to smash the door in. How dare you break into my workshop.' Rhidian stood his ground and coughed from the dust now floating in the air. 'Please leave immediately,' he ordered.

'Rhidian Fines, otherwise known as the engineer?' One of the officers spoke, his voice monotone. He stepped forward and the dust settled on his shoulders and arms.

'What? Yes,' Rhidian snapped, more annoyed now than anything else. 'You know who I am,' he said, still reeling from the disturbance. 'What is the meaning of this?' he growled again in distaste.

'You are under arrest, Rhidian Fines. Please do not try to escape. Do not move. We must restrain you,' the officer droned, and held out a pair of handcuffs.

Whilst he'd never thought of it before, Rhidian realised that each officer he'd come in contact with had the same tone – with no emotion behind the voice. Perhaps it was the way they were trained, but that didn't matter now. Rhidian soon found himself edging away. He swallowed hard, trying to get some moistness in his throat from the dry air. He couldn't believe what he was hearing. He'd always kept his nose clean and certainly wasn't a troublemaker. Why were they targeting him? He looked at Morbid, who looked directly back at him, but *not* aiding his defence.

'What? Under arrest?' he said as he stumbled, trying to make sense of it all. 'What do you mean? You can't do this,' he recoiled angrily. 'On what charge? I demand to know what I am charged with.'

The officer proceeded to readout the information on his file.

'We have been reliably informed that you have been reading illegal documents, and so we must arrest you and take you into custody.' The police officer was reading from a piece of paper which he'd produced from his pocket. He continued, 'Documents, that relate to the exiled wizard Obsidian,' the officer said, reading the charge. 'This is forbidden under Section 12 of the Valusha Law of Practice.'

Obsidian, the original ruler, had been exiled from Valusha for the use of magic. Magic had been outlawed in Valusha for many years, and was against the law to learn and practise.

'It has been reported,' the officer carried on, 'that you have been collecting documents that belonged to the exiled wizard. You have been practising magic.'

'But-but, magic, no…' Rhidian was outraged and tried to protest his point, but the officer was in full flow.

'These are the charges, please do not evade arrest or I shall have to restrain you.' The policeman moved forward in a bid to capture the engineer, but Rhidian pulled back further.

'But I only found the papers when I was looking through my work. I've only read one or two. It was an accident,' Rhidian pleaded his innocence. 'How- how did you know anyway?' He was distraught. 'I handed them over to my assistant, immediately after finding them. I gave them to Morbid to show Jenta-Lor. I didn't keep them.' Rhidian was confused and ran the memory over in his mind. He again looked at his assistant. Things weren't quite right here, and then it suddenly hit him. Morbid! Morbid must have given Jenta-Lor a different story. Rhidian was furious.

While all this was going on Morbid stood motionless in the corner and didn't utter a word. His mouth suddenly changed into a wide satisfied grin. And Rhidian realised what must have happened. He stared back and bared his teeth in contempt.

'You-you snake,' Rhidian spat, and pointed at his apprentice, his insides burning with rage. 'Why did you do this? I've done nothing but help you,' Rhidian protested, but it was no good. He had to prove his innocence. Surely Jenta-Lor would believe him over Morbid and realise it was all a set up? Yes, Jenta-Lor would soon be on his side, he was sure of it.

There was really no escape, but Rhidian took another step back and finally stopped against a table, pressing his hands on the surface. The first officer attempted to cuff him, but Rhidian struggled and pulled out of his grip. Then, the second officer loomed from behind and grasped Rhidian's wrist firmly.

'Get off me,' Rhidian said, still struggling, spittle flying from his mouth. 'You wait until Jenta-Lor hears of this.' His angry cries were wasted. 'He will have your badges.'

'The ruler, Jenta-Lor, facilitated the order,' came the response from the first officer.

'W-what?' Again, Rhidian was overwhelmed and couldn't believe what was being said to him. 'Morbid, can you help with this please?' Rhidian pleaded. 'Did you give that paperwork I found to Jenta-Lor?'

'Of course I did, you fool. I told him you've been reading everything you could get your hands on,' he said with relish – his mouth now widened to a sinister smile. 'I told him the truth, that you were practising magic.'

'But why lie?' Rhidian stammered. 'Why would you do this? I've never practised magic, you know that.'

'Don't you see, you pathetic idiot? I am in charge now. I know how to run everything in the city, and you – you will be gone forever,' he said.

'Take him away, officers. Jenta-Lor will rely on my skills from now on.' Morbid ushered the two policemen with a flick of his hand, as if brushing dust from his jacket. 'Take the wizard away, before he conjures a spell.'

'I'm not a wizard. You have to believe me – I am not a wizard,' Rhidian protested. 'Why have you done this? What did I ever do to you?' Rhidian ranted as he was forcibly taken from the premises.

'You are a fool, Rhidian Fines. Now *you* can rot in Skytraz Prison with the rest of the traitors,' he said, and laughed out loud.

'Traitor? But what have I done to betray Jenta-Lor? I am not a wizard, I'm an engineer – I fix things and build things. I have no clue about magic.' But the officers ignored his pleas. The engineer was dragged into the street. Outside he saw a vehicle waiting to take him away – the blue light on top blinking.

'Please, please don't do this.' He was still struggling when they heaved him into the back and locked the cage. He slumped to the floor. The two officers sat in the front of the car and drove off. Rhidian knew it was futile to struggle any more and settled back for a moment. He gazed through the steel bars and saw blurred images whizz past. The ride was smooth, and although he was trussed up inside a patrol car cage, he couldn't help but smile, even though this was deadly serious. The anti-magnetic technology that made the vehicle move was his invention. The floating rock in the sky that they were living on was magnetized, and the vehicle repelled it, thus powering the car along the road. He was no wizard and he was going to prove it to Jenta-Lor. As soon as they entered the station, he was going to ask to contact the ruler of Valusha and sort this out – once and for all.

But his smile turned to horror as he realised that they weren't turning right towards the Jenta Force Police Station. His stomach tightened. Where were they taking him? This wasn't right.

'Hold on, you've taken the wrong turn,' he cried. 'You've just passed Jenta Police Station. Where are you taking me?' Then, the horrific idea dropped into his mind. 'You're not taking me to Jenta Force Police Station, are you? You're taking me… straight to the docking bay and SKYTRAZ PRISON! But you can't, it's against your own laws,' he raged, but it was no use – these two zombies had their orders and that was it. 'You're not even giving me a chance to defend myself. My case has to be heard in court,' he protested again. 'You can't do this.' He tried to break free, but the bars were solid and, ironically, he'd built these cages too.

'What about my wife? I have to get word to her. Are you listening to me?' he yelled. 'You can't do this. I have to contact Mia.' The more he ranted, the more energy he used up. He rattled the cage once more, but he knew it was futile. He eventually sat back in the seat and quietly contemplated what it was he could do to get out of this situation.

The streets of Valusha were deserted at this time of night. The car silently whooshed through the quiet city. Rhidian had many thoughts rushing through his mind. How long had Morbid been planning this? Why was he doing it in the first place? Rhidian had only been helpful to him. The engineer felt at an all time low. What would Mia do when she found out?

While all this swirled in his mind the car slowed and came to a stop at the shuttle bay. The smooth transition from full speed to stop was a tranquil affair, and Rhidian remembered how much work he'd put into it to get it that way.

Now the officers took him out of the patrol car and led him to the waiting ship. He wriggled and squirmed, but it didn't matter, he was not strong enough to resist. The vessel was really a cargo ship. It lay anchored, and was bathed in lights that shone from the dock. The ship was a big structure, with a huge zeppelin-type balloon above the body, which was tethered by a lattice of metal.

When they escorted Rhidian on board, he was led to a holding pen on the vast deck. He looked around as they shunted him along. There were wooden containers chained to the deck and fixed into position with metal pins. They soon approached the cage he would be locked inside. One of the officers waited for a crewmember to open it up, and then Rhidian was pushed in.

'Please, you've got to believe me, I'm innocent. I'm not a wizard,' Rhidian again complained, but as he tried to get back out, the door was slammed shut and locked.

'Settle down.' The sailor, who had opened the door, spoke softly, and Rhidian looked at him. The man rolled his sympathetic eyes. 'Sorry mate,' he said reluctantly, 'but I can't help you. I've got my orders.' He shook his head as the police officers left the ship.

'Please don't give me any trouble,' the man concluded, 'or the captain will get annoyed and you don't want to annoy him.' Rhidian didn't answer and only peered back in silence. He watched the officers as they climbed into their patrol car and silently pulled away, and everything felt so final.

'We'll be casting off in a minute, so get some sleep, fella,' the crewman insisted. He paused. 'It'll be a while 'til we get there. There's some water in that container,' he said, whilst pointing to a bottle next to the engineer, and then he walked away, whistling as he went.

Rhidian was alone in the shadow of the balloon. He sat shivering, even though it was a warm summer's evening – the shock of everything was too much. He started to drift off into slumber, but the ship soon woke him with a start. The great engine rumbled and chugged plumes of smoke from the exhaust manifold. This was really happening, Rhidian could not quite believe it. There was a sudden shudder and a jerk, and the ship gently left the dock and began its journey.

Rhidian eased against the uncomfortable bars again and watched as Valusha, the only city he'd ever loved, got smaller. He'd never seen the city from this angle before and it was really beautiful. Tall steeples pushed out from the darkness as if waving him off. Soon, all that was left of the sky city were the diminishing lights, and eventually darkness. He felt his stomach sink.

Rhidian was still in shock, but there would be no point protesting any more; the decision was already made. What on earth was he going to do? Oh my God, he thought, Mia would be heartbroken. She wouldn't know anything about this until morning. Rhidian always worked late and she never really knew what time he would get in. What would he do without her and what would she do without him? Then a stab of sadness filled his stomach, like a dagger made of ice. Would he ever see her again?

He'd heard of Skytraz Prison many times and all the bad tales that leaked out from there. Lots of people had been sent there and never returned. A chill shot through his whole body. Would he now be one of those statistics?

The gentle sway of the ship as it glided through the air made him sleepy again; the toll of everything weighed heavily. The throb-throb-throb of the purring engine had a hypnotic effect. He'd not slept much in the last couple of days either, and felt the most relaxed for a while. The smooth vibration that rattled throughout the vessel was pure joy. He loved the sound and feel of working machinery.

Rhidian drifted off into a deep sleep, it was as if all his troubles were just a memory. He breathed shallow breaths.

He was soon awakened with a violent clang and blinding light!

'Get up,' the gruff voice of a prison guard grinded his ears.

It was daylight when Rhidian finally opened his eyes. Where was he? He couldn't work anything out for a second or two. Then it all came back. The two police officers and Morbid's contented face as he betrayed him. And the realisation that he was on his way to a prison sentence. And of course, there was his poor wife, Mia. It hadn't been a dream – this was as real as it got. Rhidian was about to enter the worst place in the world. What if he tried to appeal to the guard?

'Please, there's been some kind of mistake. I shouldn't be here. I'm not a wizard,' Rhidian tried to explain.

'Yeah-yeah, that's what they all say,' the guard chuckled and then growled, 'now get up before I drag you up.' He didn't look like a person to cross and Rhidian did as he was asked.

'Okay-okay,' Rhidian relented. He had to accept his fate for now. For some reason, Jenta-Lor and Morbid were working together on this, and Rhidian had to go along with it. But he wasn't going to let a prison trap him forever. Before he'd even left the cargo ship and entered god-knows-what, he swore he would escape. But no one had ever escaped from Skytraz Prison, or so he'd heard. Rhidian Fines, the engineer, was determined that he would be the first one to do it.

Chapter 2
Skytraz Prison

Skytraz Prison was originally a rock that had broken away from a larger body in the universe. It appeared in the sky and ships were sent to investigate. The rock was huge in size (a fragment the size of a planet) and lay suspended in mid-air by some unknown force. Obsidian staked a claim and populated it. He realised that hardened criminals had to be put somewhere far away from the innocent. So, he organised a prison to be built on the rock and the criminal element were sent there. There was no escape from Skytraz, and no one had ever tried.

Valusha itself, also another suspended mass but fully populated, was much larger than Skytraz. In fact, it was a huge city where the new ruler, Jenta-Lor, was in charge and the people were made to work hard and to pay heavy taxes. Jenta-Lor lived the lifestyle of a king.

*****

Rhidian stepped off the cargo vessel and onto the jetty. Everything became real in a matter of moments. The handcuffs jangled on his wrists, reminding him of his sorry predicament. This added extra tension, making the pit of his stomach twist like a wrung-out rag. He swallowed hard and took deep breaths. He felt his whole life had been crushed overnight. He took a few moments to gather his thoughts, until he was unceremoniously jarred from them with a sharp pain.

'This way – move!' the guard insisted with a grunt, and struck Rhidian in the small of his back with the butt of his rifle. Rhidian winced as he lurched forward. He moved reluctantly, but obediently, like a scolded dog. He'd never been ordered to do anything he didn't want to do before, but things had changed considerably in his life.

Rhidian walked along the long, wooden platform, which was set on the very perimeter of Skytraz Prison. The platform seemed to float on a cushion of air, but was actually fixed underneath with huge steel struts that held it all in place.

Everything was open, which was unusual for a place where you would expect some kind of confinement for the prisoners, he thought. In fact there were no large fences or high walls to imprison anyone. There was, however, a metre-high perimeter boundary fence. It wasn't so much a deterrent as a marker. This must have been put there to let the prisoners know what danger lay ahead. Because beyond it, there was about five metres of rock surface... and beyond that... nothing but thin air! Literally, there was nowhere to escape. It was a long way to the sea below, and that would mean certain death as a result.

As Rhidian shuffled along, he gazed out into the blue expanse – it was an amazing view, easily as lovely as the views from Valusha. There were two swallows flitting through the sky, playing games with each other. Rhidian never felt so jealous of freedom in all his life. He wished he could take flight and leave this awful place right now.

Was there any escape from a prison this high up? He pondered on that idea. Unless... he could get on board a supply ship. He stared over his shoulder at the vessel that had dropped him off as he turned to enter the first building. It was so near, but of no use at this time. There was also another docked next to it, but he didn't get a chance to take a longer look at it as the guard pushed him again. The engineer stared ahead and craned his neck to take in the whole scale of the prison.

It was impressive to say the least and depressing at the same time. He stood a moment, taking in the expanse of his new dwelling and was soon brought back to reality.

'Stop dawdling and move,' the prison guard grunted. He was impatient and rude and gave Rhidian another tap with the rifle, which hurt but he didn't show it, and just gritted his teeth. Rhidian was *guided* towards the entrance. 'Tough guy, huh?' he heard the guard mumble – followed by a little chuckle.

Rhidian was then led to the Processing Centre where all prisoners went to get booked in. He was told to stand on a crisscross, which was painted in yellow on the floor. Another officer behind a counter confronted him. Rhidian had nothing with him to hand over, only the clothes he wore. They hadn't given him a chance to change or pick anything up that he might need. He again thought of Mia at this time and this made him feel more dejected. Rhidian couldn't remember the last time he'd ever felt this alone. He could feel a well of tears building, but swallowed back hard and reasserted his composure. The last thing he wanted was to show he was afraid and vulnerable, and that wouldn't do in here.

The supplies officer handed him a bundle of clothes with a pair of shiny boots nestled on top and ordered him to change. An officer with a bunch of keys unlocked the bracelet and removed it.

'Don't be thinking of escaping now, there's nowhere to go,' the prison guard said with a grin, as he whispered the last part with relish. Rhidian rubbed his wrists – the steel rings had already left indentations. The orange boiler suit was very unattractive and also too big, but he didn't dare complain.

The officer enjoyed giving him a look of contempt. Rhidian again said nothing – he was too scared to react. He quickly stripped and put on the prison-issue clothes. He then placed his own clothes in a waiting tray. He looked forlornly at them as they were put on a trolley.

'You won't be needing those again – you're our special guest now,' the supplies officer said and added a smirk. The man with the keys slipped the cuffs back on – the weight of the metal tugged at his wrists.

'Right, through here – Prisoner 8317,' a different officer beckoned, his brown, unforgiving eyes fixed on Rhidian. All the guards he'd come into contact with so far held no friendly expression of any kind. Rhidian was only a number now, and not even a name. What was he doing here? He didn't deserve this. He didn't belong here, everything seemed so wrong.

'Move, weed,' the officer said in a low snarl, and again poked Rhidian in the back. Another guard had joined them as he walked along the open floor. These guards were trying to provoke him, but he wasn't going to get into trouble this soon. I will find a way of escape, he thought defiantly, and that made him feel better for a second or two.

The guards took him through a number of security doors – Rhidian tried to remember the sequence. Each entrance clicked open and clicked shut behind him – the tinny sound pierced his ears and numbed his senses. He could hear his own footsteps slopping along on the polished floor. The air smelled of a mixture of disinfectant and floor polish. He was marched to yet another counter, where the second supplies officer in charge was giving out bathroom necessities. They made Rhidian stand behind a yellow *line* this time.

'Just there,' the guard said – he had a softer tone than the others. He looked much older too, and Rhidian thought he was probably ready for retirement. Rhidian felt a large hand roughly grip his shoulder and pull him. He realised he was too close to the partition and was yanked back to the yellow line. He almost fell over but managed to keep his balance – this shoving around had already got tedious, but what could he do?

This particular officer at the counter gave him a warm smile. Rhidian didn't expect that. He felt as though he was standing in front of the head teacher back at school. He didn't smile back and kept his expression blank. The store man probably understood, especially dealing with inmates on a daily basis.

'*These* are your personal possessions. *Do not* lose them,' he said, emphasizing the first two words. 'You won't get another set,' said the store man. He placed a toothbrush, toothpaste, a comb and a bar of soap on top of brown bedding and a towel, which were neatly folded on the counter.

'You're all set, 8317. Enjoy your stay,' the old man said with a wink, which made the engineer a bit more relaxed. But that soon changed.

The prison guard who'd brought him in, and the second guard with the keys, continued further into Skytraz, nudging the prisoner to move again. They were greeted with yet more guards with jingly-jangly keys, to open and close yet more doors. How many doors were there in this place? Rhidian had already lost count. This was getting monotonous, but he had to get used to it. He could feel his will to live slowly fading away with every step.

Eventually, he was escorted into the main prison area, where the light was partially swallowed by the geometry of the place. He could hear the caged prisoners jeering and chanting in the background. This, he felt, was the most scary part of the whole thing. It brought the complete prison experience to the front of his mind.

'Come on, this way,' the guard seemed to squeak. 'We haven't got all day.' He led him down to a lower level. It was even darker down here than the place he'd just been. It was also a lot quieter too. This really scared him. Where were they taking him now?

Rhidian's feet squeaked on the freshly polished floor – the sound ripped through the establishment like a rapier cutting into tin. He could feel his body tremble and the stiff collar of the prison suit stuck in his neck, irritating his skin.

The guard stopped and released him to another guard. This one held a clipboard. His face was just as stern and lifeless as the rest. Were they as miserable as the prisoners?

He said simply, '8317,' and pointed to a darkened set of cells along a corridor. Rhidian found it hard not to be called by his name. 'This will be your home for a short while,' the officer said. Rhidian again said nothing and followed the leader.

This level was different to the others above. It only had two compartments down here. To his right there was a long wall and the cells were located at the end on the left.

The guard stopped, opened the steel door and looked inside, shaking his head. He then took off Rhidian's handcuffs. Rhidian looked at the darkened room in which he'd be confined and a sinking feeling filled his guts.

'This is where you'll stay for now. It's only temporary. Have fun with your little friend,' the guard sniggered as he pushed him inside.

Rhidian was confused. 'Little friend,' he mumbled, but didn't know what the prison guard had meant. 'Oh, rats,' he assumed and shuddered as he looked on the ground for evidence. He swallowed hard and clenched his eyes shut when he heard the cell door lock behind him!

Chapter 3
The Stranger

Rhidian stood still, holding his bedding and bathroom utensils and stared at the small toilet and hand basin. There was only really one piece of furniture besides the beds and that was a tiny cupboard above the basin. He presumed that's where he had to place his bathroom kit. The look of the cell surprised him too, because he was expecting the basin and toilet to be stained and filthy, but they weren't. In fact, they were actually really clean and stain free. The whole cell was neat and tidy too.

He was still pondering on the "little friend" comment that the guard had said and assumed he meant a mouse, or a rat! Rhidian shivered again.

'Oh well, let's make the most of it,' he mumbled. 'At least I have a cell to myself.'

'Who are you?' a voice whispered, cutting through the stillness of the room. Rhidian froze and tightly gripped his bedding. He thought he was alone but there was definitely someone else in here. He was shocked – why couldn't he see anyone? He was stood in the middle of the room.

He quickly checked the top bunk. He looked at the surface of the bed and grinned. If there were anyone in there, he had to be small and flat to fit under the blanket – it was definitely empty.

Rhidian leaned back and gave a quick check underneath. Nothing there, he felt stupid. Perhaps he was imagining it? After all, the shock of being arrested and shuffled off to prison – he rolled his head from side-to-side, weighing everything up. No wonder he was confused.

Deciding it was his imagination, Rhidian placed his kit on the top bunk bed. He relaxed and sighed.

'I said, who are you?'

Rhidian stiffened. It was the voice again, but where was it coming from? Maybe there was someone in the next cell. He couldn't call out – he didn't want the guards coming back – so he resisted.

He looked around. The room itself was made up of three solid walls and a framework of bars at the front. Rhidian was totally confused now, but thought he'd better be polite and answer. He shook his head in the disbelief at what he was doing.

'I-I'm Rhidian,' he stuttered. 'Who are you?' Rhidian was speaking directly to the wall.

'Why are you talking to the wall, Rhidian?' the voice mocked, and then a head popped up from under the bottom bunk. Rhidian looked down, his eyes wide. The man pulled himself out and Rhidian had to shuffle to one side. Then the old man stood up and the engineer could look him directly in the eye.

'Wh-o are you?' Rhidian asked nervously, hoping he wasn't a murderer or someone with a troubled mind, or both!

'There's no need to be afraid of me, young man,' he said, and gave a broad and cheery smile.

'I'm n-not afraid,' Rhidian retorted with as much strength in his voice as he could muster.

'Tell that to your face then,' the old man replied with a wicked glint in his eye. He was about five feet two, with wiry white hair and a trim, well-groomed dark brown beard, which was a total contrast. He looked to be in his sixties, but it was difficult to tell. He was wearing the prison-issue orange boiler suit: the same as Rhidian had been handed earlier. What would this guy have normally worn on the outside? Rhidian was thinking maybe a suit or, at the very least, trousers and a dress shirt. He seemed well presented and kept himself in shape – he didn't look overweight.

'Really, there's no need to worry, my boy,' the stranger carried on. Rhidian was still reeling from the sight of someone popping from under the bed. 'My name is Rebus.' He stuck out his hand in welcome. Rhidian reached out and tentatively shook hands.

'I-I'm sorry I don't know which bed is yours – mean as you were here first,' Rhidian stammered. 'I'm Rhidian,' he repeated.

'I know, you've already told me. I'm on the top, take the bottom,' Rebus insisted, gesturing with a sweep of his hand. Rhidian then realised he'd put his belongings on Rebus' bed and removed them instantly. He then placed his bedding in the centre of the mattress on the bottom bunk.

'Can I put my stuff in there?' Rhidian asked politely, pointing to the small cabinet above the washbasin.

'Go ahead,' Rebus obliged. It was as spotless on the inside as out. There was a space next to the old gent's toothbrush and toothpaste. He put his stuff next to them. He thought that if he'd looked in there earlier, he would have realised someone else was in the cell, but there again he wasn't expecting someone under the bed.

'What are you in for, Rhidian?' Rebus questioned directly. 'Not murder I hope?' the old man quipped with a penetrating stare.

'No, no – God no,' Rhidian answered. 'I-I read a document by mistake, and I'm being punished for it,' he confessed, still jaded. 'W-why were you under the bed?' he asked curiously.

'Ah, you think I'm a bit unhinged?' Rebus reacted abruptly, his wild blue eyes peering at him through the dimly lit room.

41

'No, well, err...' Rhidian didn't know how to answer.

'*They* think I'm mad,' Rebus rounded, emphasising the *they*, while pointing in the direction of where the guards had just brought Rhidian in.

'What – the prison officers?' Rhidian retorted absentmindedly, looking in the same direction.

'Yes, of course the prison officers, who else? We're in a prison, aren't we?' he snapped, rolling his eyes.

'All right-all right, I was only asking,' Rhidian shot back. 'Boy you're touchy.'

'Sorry, Rhidian, you'll be touchy too after spending time in here.' Rebus softened. 'I hide under the bed to make them think I'm mad, and that way normally they don't put anyone in with me for long. I like the solitude.'

'Oh, I see, clever tactics.' Rhidian arched his brow in appreciation. 'I hate it here already.'

'Tell me, Rhidian, I'm assuming you've come from Valusha?' Rebus said, returning to the original conversation.

'Yes,' Rhidian answered and a stab of homesickness gripped his stomach. Mia popped into his mind and he tried to think of something else to keep control. It seemed so long ago that he'd seen her, but it was only the day before when he'd left for work.

'And you've been arrested for reading a document you say?' Rebus seemed really interested. 'Curious,' he added with pursed lips.

'Yes, but I didn't mean to read it,' Rhidian said in his defence. 'And that was it – I was sent here without even giving me a chance to prove my innocence.'

'What sort of document was it that you were reading? It must have been something really offensive or top secret,' Rebus dug deeper.

'Why-why do you want to know?' Rhidian uttered, feeling like he was a specimen in a lab. 'You seem very interested in my business. Are you working for the prison warden?' Rhidian looked at Rebus with contempt.

Rebus broke into the biggest belly laugh and almost doubled over.

'No-no, of course I'm not, sorry,' Rebus said, still chuckling, but realised Rhidian was confused. 'Okay, it's very important that you tell me where you came across this document? Please, I'm honestly not working for the prison in any capacity. I just really need to know,' Rebus asked and paused for the answer.

Rhidian thought it over for a moment and decided it wouldn't hurt to tell. What could they do to him? He was captured now anyway.

'What difference does it make now?' he relented. 'I'm already in here, aren't I? I found it in my workshop,' he said not holding back.

Rebus arched his eyebrow at the mention of the workshop.

'Please,' he said, and looked very serious. He ran his tongue along his lips. 'Was it written by someone called Obsidian?' Rebus said, studying Rhidian's eyes.

Rhidian glared back.

'Yes, yes it was, why?' Rhidian hissed excitedly, almost in a whisper.

Rebus' eyes lit up at the revelation, just like a child who had found a hoard of silver coins. 'I knew it,' he said and a huge smile erupted across his tired face.

'You knew this man?' Rhidian was intrigued. 'How could you know Obsidian?'

'Knew him? Of course I knew him,' Rebus exclaimed. 'He was the ruler of Valusha and the most powerful wizard I'd ever met. That was until he was exiled.' Rebus' eyes burned with real hatred. 'If you found his documents then you must have been in *his* workshop?'

'Yes, I presume I was. I'm an engineer and was looking for some plans for a job I was working on and came across the document. I only took a glimpse, but as soon as Jenta-Lor found out about it…' Rebus cut in on Rhidian.

'Jenta-Lor is an evil excuse of a man. He's ruthless and single-minded. He needs to be stricken from power.' Rebus went from warm and friendly to agitated and bitter in the matter of a few seconds.

'I agree, Rebus. He imprisoned me for no reason at all really. I have, well err, had, an apprentice called Morbid. He told Jenta-Lor that I'd read the documents on magic, and that *I* was a wizard too. Now I've been imprisoned and he's got my job.' Rhidian was sounding bitter too. 'Why are you here?' He looked at Rebus.

'I'm also a wizard. I was under Obsidian's command,' Rebus said truthfully.

Rhidian looked as if he'd swallowed something that needed to come back up.

'A real wizard?' Rhidian exclaimed. It took him a moment or two to take it in.

'Yeah, I'm a real wizard. That's why they leave me alone in here. They think I can still do harm and perform magic. So neither the prisoners nor the guards want anything to do with me. And I help it a little by acting eccentric,' Rebus explained.

Rhidian had read about wizards, but when he'd moved into Valusha they'd all gone. He then peered back at Rebus. 'Why don't you escape from here?' he quizzed, his voice getting louder. 'Wizards make magic, don't they? You could conjure a spell and blow the cell doors off.' He was really sceptical, and wondered if this man was actually telling the truth.

'Shh…' Rebus' face tightened and he put his finger to his lips. 'Don't give any information away in this place. The less they know the better.' He again pointed towards the end of the corridor.

'Oops, okay, sorry.' Rhidian lowered his voice and looked a little sheepish. Perhaps he is telling the truth, Rhidian pondered. There were rules to this place as anywhere else, and as a newbie he would probably have to learn them right away.

'I can't use my magic in here, there's a seal around the prison which stopped my powers from working,' Rebus explained. Rhidian's mind went into overdrive. How would such a seal work, especially where magic was involved?

'Who put the seal on the prison?' Rhidian asked.

'Jenta-Lor. Jenta-Lor has taken it upon himself to own this prison and Valusha,' Rebus revealed.

'Are you talking about some kind of "damper field"? I've been an engineer for years, and I wouldn't have a clue as to how to build a damper field to stop the use of magic. Whoever has done such a thing would have to be a wizard too, for that kind of power?' Rhidian assumed. 'But wizards aren't allowed in Valusha, are they?'

'That's exactly what I thought,' Rebus reasoned. 'He's claiming he's not but I can't use my magic, and that would mean that a wizard is running this place *and* Valusha. So, Jenta-Lor has fooled everyone,' Rebus realised.

'How many wizards were there in Valusha, besides you and Obsidian?' Rhidian asked. And where are they now?' Rhidian was very interested. Where there were good wizards, there was hope, he assumed.

'Only two more as far as I can remember, but there may have been others,' Rebus retorted. 'But they escaped the same time as Obsidian. There could be some who have kept themselves secret. I was rendered unconscious when they caught me, so I couldn't use my magic. Anyway, it wouldn't have mattered because the damper was already in use,' Rebus said bitterly, still beating himself up on being captured. 'I've been here ever since.'

Why haven't they come back for you, Obsidian and the others?' Rhidian queried.

'They can't use their magic and don't want to be captured either probably. They were lucky to escape the first time,' Rebus said. 'They must be scattered in different places. As for Obsidian, he's disappeared without a trace. I haven't heard from any of them.' Rebus was obviously feeling that he'd been abandoned.

'Rebus, look, I need to get out of here,' Rhidian confessed. 'I have to get away from here and find my wife, Mia. She's in danger in Valusha. Once

I've done that, she and I can go somewhere safe and live out our lives in another place far from here.'

'I need to get out of here, too, and find Obsidian,' Rebus said in reply. 'He needs to be back in charge of the city. And then you won't have to move away. You and your wife can stay and live in peace in Valusha again.'

'But if you can't use your powers,' Rhidian said, 'how are you going to manage it? This place is a fortress from what I've seen and, more importantly, nowhere to escape to. We're on a floating rock!'

'I've been locked up here quite a while.' Rhidian could see the bitterness in his eyes. 'I know everything that goes on in here, from memory. I've been studying this place for a couple of years, waiting for someone to help me escape. I know all the routines of the guards and the blueprint of the prison. I only need to break out and get hold of a sky ship and find Obsidian. The sky ship that brought you here will be leaving at ten o'clock tonight. I need to be on that ship,' Rebus stated. 'Once out of here, I can regain my magic and find where my master is, then convince him to come back.'

'What? Tonight? You want to escape tonight?' Rhidian felt a twinge of excitement. 'What then? Where will we go?' he asked.

'Well, hopefully round up the rest of the wizards who were exiled. Once we have our powers back we can take back Valusha and restore peace. Jenta-Lor has a lot to answer for and he needs to be imprisoned.'

'I can help,' Rhidian chipped in. 'I really can,' he gushed with delight.

'How?' Rebus was wide eyed. 'What can you do?'

'For one, I can pilot a sky ship. I'm an engineer, remember? I've messed about with sky ships on Valusha. And... I'm also a locksmith too, which Jenta-Lor doesn't know about,' Rhidian said with a grin. 'I don't want to stay here any longer than I have to.'

'You are exactly what I've been looking for.' Rebus' face was filled with hope and joy. 'But it's not going to be easy. I have a plan for just two people, so...' Rebus was interrupted!

'I can help, too.' The voice came from beyond the room.

Rebus and Rhidian stopped talking and were filled with fear. What they'd been speaking about could now be all in vain. Someone else was listening, but whom? Rebus swallowed hard and stared at Rhidian. He thought the next cell was empty. How did this person get in without his knowledge? How stupid was he to not know? Damn it, he cursed himself.

'Who are you? What have you heard?' Rebus rasped with anger. 'Come on, out with it, right now.'

'I'm Red, sir. I didn't mean to, but I heard everything.' The tone was of a younger person. A gentle, timid voice bled through the wall. 'I've just come in here today and they put me in this cell alone. Let me help you. I want to escape with you too, please,' he said with desperation in his voice. 'I won't tell, honest. I need to get out of here. I don't think I can make it if I stay in here any longer.'

The boy seemed genuine enough.

'How come I didn't hear you?' Rebus pressed, still not convinced that this person was trustworthy.

'I don't know. Maybe you were sleeping? It was quiet when I was put here and I didn't know you were there, until Rhidian came in, that is,' the boy called back in little higher than a whisper.

'Is there definitely no one else in there with you?' Rebus probed. 'Tell me, boy.' His tone was commanding.

'No one. I was brought into the prison last night and put in another cell. Then they put me in here,' he explained. 'There was no one down here when they brought me in. I'm telling the truth, sir,' Red explained. That made sense to Rebus because he'd been taken to the exercise yard earlier.

'How old are you, son?' Rhidian asked with curiosity.

'I'm fifteen, sir,' he said with a shake in his voice.

'What the devil is a fifteen-year-old boy doing in here with the adults?' Rhidian asked Rebus.

'It doesn't matter to Jenta-Lor how old you are,' Rebus replied.

'Why are you in here, son?' Rebus called in a friendlier tone.

'I don't know. I haven't done anything wrong,' Red answered honestly. 'But they arrested me anyway.' This struck a chord with Rhidian, as he'd been abducted too.

'Where's your family?' Rhidian added.

'They died years ago and I've been moving around the city on my own,' he told them.

'That makes sense, too,' Rhidian said. 'Jenta-Lor doesn't want strays cluttering up his city. They either end up here or disappear for good.'

'OK, sit tight, Red, and keep quiet. We're all going to escape tonight, but we haven't much time,' Rebus explained with eyes half open, knowing that he had to trust Rhidian and Red now. 'Let me think. They'll leave you two here for a couple of days. These are just holding cells. That means we'll be left alone after we've eaten in the Mess Hall. We will have to break out then, under cover of darkness. They won't be expecting the

51

"new fish" to escape on the first night.' Rebus' eyes flashed and a grin filled his mouth. 'They won't expect anyone to escape at all!' And he laughed.

Chapter 4
Mia

She rolled over and automatically reached out to the spot where Rhidian normally slept. Her hand flattened on the cool empty space on the mattress where the duvet had been pulled away. Half asleep, she puzzled as to where he was. She lazily raised her eyelids and gradually focused. She took in a deep breath and let out a long-winded yawn. Mia smacked her lips together and cleared her dry throat.

'Rhidian? Rhidian?' she repeated through the still darkness of the room, her voice croaky. 'Where are you?' But he wasn't there and that was unusual. He did work late most nights, but not this late. She lay there for a few seconds, pondering. This was odd, she thought.

Suddenly the quietness of the night was violently interrupted by a heavy banging at the door downstairs. Mia sat bolt upright in bed and immediately thought the worst.

'Oh my God. Rhidian!' she called out. She got up, and slipped on her dressing gown and in haste forgot her slippers. Her heart raced as she hurried downstairs, not knowing what fate lay ahead. She felt short of breath and by the time she got to the hallway she was gasping for air.

Mia turned on the light and suddenly thought that it could be anybody trying to get in. But there again, burglars wouldn't knock and raise the alarm. Also, Rhidian would have his own key. But she was quite frightened by now and held back. She stood quietly in the cool of the passageway panting, trying to figure out what to do. She tried to control her breathing by taking shorter puffs.

'W-who's there?' she trembled, her throat still hoarse and weak.

'Mia Fines?' the voice boomed from the other side. Jenta Police, she realised straight away. What did they want with her at this time of night?

'Y-Yes,' Mia gasped. 'What do yo...' but she didn't have time to finish.

'We are Jenta Force police officers – open the door immediately or we will be forced to break it down.' She was scared and didn't know what to do. Where was Rhidian when she needed him? Why were they breaking down her door? What had Rhidian done? What had she done? Her head was filled with all kinds of theories.

'Okay, hold on,' she said, her whole body shaking from shock. 'Just a minute, I have to get dressed.' She stalled for time, but it didn't matter, it was too late anyway.

Suddenly there were two, heavy thudding sounds. The first shook the complete frame and made Mia scream. The second one, the door gave way and in burst two police officers. Mia was terrified and tried to make her way back upstairs; her instinct was telling her that this situation was all wrong.

'Mia Fines, you are under arrest. You must come with us,' one of the police officers said as he lunged and grabbed her arm, which spun her round. He then slipped handcuffs on both her wrists. Terrified, she peered at his face, but it was obscured with a visor. All she could make out were the eyes, which were reddened and lifeless. That scared her more than anything.

'Please-please, don't,' she squeaked, and tried to wriggle out of the steel bands, but there was no escape. She was hysterical now, tears rolling down her cheeks. 'But I haven't done anything wrong,' she pleaded. 'Please, why have you come here? Please can I put proper clothes on?'

The two policemen didn't answer and led her straight outside – still barefoot. There was a vehicle waiting, its painful blue flashing lights stabbed at her eyes, making her squint. She lifted her hands to block the pulsing brightness. The officer pushed her towards the car, rough in his endeavour. The back door was already opened as Mia was heaved inside, still wrestling with the cuffs.

'Please stop. Where are you taking me?' The car sped off with her sobbing and terrified in the back.

Valusha was a vast city and Mia was taken to the heart of it. The vehicle zoomed through the empty streets – the patrol car was the very same one which had only earlier taken her husband, Rhidian, to the ship. The same officers now held his wife and had special orders to place her inside the vehicle, while Rhidian had been thrown in the cage at the back.

Mia stopped struggling; there was actually no point. She worked out that it would all be a mistake and she would protest to Jenta-Lor and everything would be back to normal again, she hoped. This was obviously a complete misunderstanding. Rhidian must be there too, she thought.

The police car silently whooshed along the roads. The car stopped outside Jenta-Lor's mansion and this made Mia feel a little more relaxed. She'd spoken to the ruler on previous occasions when he'd held parties. He invited his most experienced engineer and his lovely wife, she recalled. Mia remembered that charm exuded from Jenta-Lor, like a dripping, wet sponge. This will soon be sorted out, she gasped and pursed her lips. She rested a little more easily into the seat. She'd see Rhidian soon enough.

The large steel gates silently opened, rolling away and disappearing into the walls each side; it seemed to take ages. Mia couldn't help gazing at the splendour of it all. The dainty, coloured lights that lined the way; it was beautiful.

The car drove off and snaked its way up the twisty road that led to the main entrance. Finally, the car drew up outside the house and the door was opened for Mia to get out. At least she wasn't going to the Jenta-Lor police headquarters, but why she was in handcuffs? She had no idea.

'What am I doing here?' she asked with a little more courage, and tried to wrap her dressing gown tightly around her body; it was difficult with the handcuffs. She felt vulnerable and silly still dressed in her nightclothes and the ground was cold on her bare feet.

'Could somebody please tell me what's going on?' she pleaded to her captors, but they didn't respond. It was at that point that she realised that all Jenta Force officers only seemed to respond to instructions, as if they were in some kind of trance. She relented and waited for whatever was about to happen.

The building was vast and in the light of the entrance the walls looked a pale off-white or cream. Still not uttering anything, the two officers escorted Mia past the front door and into the foyer. It felt more comfortable to step on the smooth marble floor. The grounds outside were rough and grated on the balls of her feet.

'Take off the handcuffs,' Morbid said, as he stood, obviously waiting for her to arrive. The officers did as they were asked. 'You may go,' Morbid squeaked. The officers turned and exited the building. Mia stood rubbing her wrists and wincing. She raised her eye level to Rhidian's assistant and pulled on her robe again, feeling vulnerable in her night wear.

'Did they hurt you, my dear?' he said, his eyes dark and uncaring, contradicting the words.

'N-no, not really,' she replied. 'I-I...' but nothing else came out.

'Please, follow me. His Excellency will see you now,' he instructed and turned away.

Mia, confused and nervous, followed Morbid obediently. What was going on? Where was Rhidian? Everything was swimming through her head at the same time. She walked, taking in the surroundings. The ceilings were high and beautifully decorated, the walls smooth with exquisite paintings set at exactly the same distance from each other. She'd remembered this from her previous time here.

Morbid came to a door and stopped before giving it a gentle tap. Mia stood waiting behind him, her heart beating hard. She didn't have a good feeling about this at all.

'Come,' a muffled voice emitted from beyond the door. Morbid twisted the gold handle and disappeared inside, closing the door behind him.

Mia waited patiently. It wasn't cold, but her body trembled as if it was. This was ridiculous; she was standing in Jenta-Lor's stately home in the middle of the night, dressed in her bed wear. She took a deep breath and tried to prepare herself with some diplomatic questions. But none of them would reveal how she really felt: confused and annoyed.

Soon, Morbid opened the door and called her inside. Mia took another deep breath, and tried to control her tremble as she tentatively walked over the threshold and into an audience with the ruler of Valusha, Jenta-Lor!

Chapter 5
Escape Plan

All prisoners were led back to their cells after an hour in the exercise yard.

Earlier, it had been a strange and scary experience in the mess hall. Everyone seemed to be looking at the new recruits. Rhidian sat eating his food nervously; this was one experience he would have to get used to, unless he could actually escape. Red had the same problem in a different part of the canteen. Once they were outside in the "general population area", Rhidian met Red for the first time.

The engineer gazed at the lad with a sense of sadness. He was only a boy, blond hair, skinny frame and the look of innocence. The other inmates were staring at both of them, but with Rebus as a chaperon, the other prisoners kept their distance. Wizards definitely held an air of authority even as a prisoner. Rebus was right.

Rhidian was scared, but this boy must be terrified, he thought, especially in a prison full of adults. Rhidian couldn't protect him in the long run – he didn't even know if he could protect himself in this hellhole. Rebus wouldn't be around all the time, so they would have to help each other, and neither of them would be able to defend themselves against a seasoned gang of inmates!

The buzzer sounded for everyone to go back to the cells and this gave a small jolt of relief. Red and Rhidian couldn't wait to leave this place and return to the safety of their section. Finally, Rebus and Rhidian were locked back in together. Red was also put on his own again in the cell next to them. He was still worried as to whether they would put someone else in with him. Rebus was just relieved that they were all together, so the plan still had a chance.

'Don't worry, kid, you'll soon have a cell mate in the morning,' the guard said and grinned at the boy. Red began to sob and this seemed to give the guard a dark thrill – he laughed as he locked the door. They listened as the heavy footsteps faded into the distance. They waited until the last tinkle of keys pierced the air and the door was finally locked. That was it – they were all left in silence. The next thing to happen was the light in the main corridor extinguished and all was in darkness.

It was too quiet and Red couldn't stand it any longer and had to speak.

'What's happening, guys?' he whispered with a tremble in his voice.

'Shh, just sit quietly for a while, Red,' Rebus hissed. 'Walls have ears and we don't need anyone listening.' Red did as he was told. He sat with his heart pumping and his body tense.

They waited quite a while and that made the boy even more distraught. The last guard made his final rounds an hour later. That hour seemed endless – every second seemed to dance around and tease them. Once the beam from the guards' torch distinguished and the lock clicked, the plan was put into action.

'Right, that's it until morning. It's eight o'clock now and we have two hours before the ship sails. The only reason any guard will come during the night is when there's a problem. They don't want to stay in here any longer than they have to. We have to be on that ship before the crew start boarding at nine-thirty, or it'll be all for nothing. We have to get on board while it's hopefully empty,' Rebus said, with all his experience of the prison and timetable.

'But, what if he comes back on the off chance, though?' Rhidian was looking for all the things that could go wrong.

'Then we will get caught, pure and simple,' Rebus replied bluntly. 'There are no guarantees with this. No one has ever escaped Skytraz Prison before and there's good reason. We're above the clouds and there's no other way off this place. I suspect that there haven't been many attempts because I've not heard of any since I've been here. So they won't be expecting us to try. Right, I'm hoping that the guards are playing cards or sleeping until the morning. They used to make a patrol once in the early hours but that stopped some time ago. People just accept their fate that there's no escape from this place.'

'What happens now, Rebus?' Rhidian pushed for some kind of answer.

The old wizard got up and walked towards the corner where the wall met the bars. He began picking at the surface of the cement. Rhidian could only hear the scratching, but still looked on, intrigued. Rebus dug at the seam between the steel and cement.

'What are you...?' Rhidian was about to ask, but was stopped from going any further with his enquiry.

'Shh,' the old man uttered. Rebus stabbed at the wall with his finger and slithers of cement fell to the floor. The old wizard had dug a seam the length of a pencil and the floor was a small mess of debris. He then pulled out something. Rhidian was burning inside with curiosity. Rebus turned to Rhidian, grasped his arm in the dense blackness and pressed something in his hand. Rhidian flinched at first, but played with what he'd been given. To his utter amazement, there were two pieces of metal – long and slim.

'Can you pick the lock with those?' he uttered casually. Rhidian examined the metal with more urgency – the length, thickness and also the ends. To his surprise, one end was offset at the tip, like a dentist's instrument and the other, a straight point. These would be perfect for manoeuvring the tumblers inside the lock, he thought.

'They'll be just right, Rebus. I hope, anyway,' Rhidian expressed, totally in awe of the wizard's ingenuity. 'How on earth did you hide them so well?'

'That's not important now. We have to move quickly in order to get to the boat,' Rebus said with urgency.

Rhidian wasted no more time and knelt in front of the keyhole. He fumbled in the darkness of the cell and felt for the lock. He'd done this a million times before, but never blind and never under so much pressure.

He took a few shallow breaths, closed his eyes and tried to clear his mind of everything except the lock. He smoothly felt his way inside the mechanism with the needle and for a short while tinkered about blindly. When he was satisfied, he used the other curve-ended pin and flicked at the barrel.

Rhidian's face would have been a picture if the lights were on. He twisted and contorted with every movement of the skeletal keys. It was hard trying to feel the movement – he had to be at one with the instruments. Rebus stood behind, hoping this would work. If not, then all the years of waiting would be in vain. Rhidian grunted and groaned as he toyed with the lock. Come on, come on, he urged himself silently.

'How's it going?' Rebus rasped in his ear.

'Shh,' Rhidian replied, trying to concentrate. He didn't need the distraction, not at this point. After about two minutes there was a click… and then another, and Rhidian stepped back. 'Phew,' the engineer gasped as he pulled the door to one side, quietly easing it on its rail. He could hear the restrained, child-like laughter of Rebus in the dark.

'You did it, you beauty,' he gushed and shook Rhidian's shoulder in admiration.

'Okay, I'll sort Red's next,' Rhidian said with confidence. He stepped outside and felt his way to Red's cell. He stooped down again and started the procedure all over again. This time it didn't take long, a few moments and the door slid open.

Now, all three were in the passageway, groping along the wall. Rebus led as Rhidian and Red followed up the rear. Red thought he would pass out – the dangerous excitement of being caught was overwhelming.

The group soon found their way to the steps. Rebus moved up to the next floor and came to a stop at the top. He knew there was a steel door to tackle. The others settled next to him and all three stood for a moment, listening. All seemed quiet; well, they hoped it was anyway.

'Rhidian,' Rebus uttered in the dark. Rhidian knew exactly what he had to do. He worked his magic on this door too and within a few moments, and after a little struggle, it gave way with a crack. Red was about to walk through when Rebus grabbed his shoulder.

'Hold on, lad,' Rebus whispered. 'This leads to the open part of the prison,' he said gravely. 'We've got to be deathly quiet. If anyone hears us, anyone, prisoners or guards, it's all over.' Rebus' tone was dire, and was totally understandable to the two new inmates. 'Follow me quickly to the kitchen and try not to make any sound at all,' he repeated. 'Is everyone ready?' Rebus could hear the rustle of movement and assumed they were nodding.

They gently pushed the door open the rest of the way and closed it behind them. They were on the south side of the prison, facing the end row of aisles. From this vantage point, the prisoners couldn't see them. And the escapees were far enough away from the guardhouse not to cause suspicion.

Keeping low, they slowly edged their way to the kitchen, following the wizard. They quickly realised that the soles of their boots screeched on the newly polished floor. Rebus stopped, and so did they. He slipped his hand in his pocket and handed Rhidian a small block of wax.

'Rub it on the soles and heels of your boots,' he hissed, 'and hand it to Red.' They did as he'd asked, and quickly handed the wax back to Rebus. The squeak was gone, but the ground now was slippery. So stealthily, and as safely as they could, they made their way along the floor.

The open space was vast and the crew felt small scurrying around in the darkness. As they approached the kitchen door, Rhidian stepped forward to do his stuff as expected. He'd only been tampering with the lock for a few seconds when suddenly Rebus gripped his shoulder, tightly. Rhidian stopped immediately, wondering why.

Then he realised; there were footsteps fast approaching and panic ensued. The fear of being caught halfway through a jailbreak terrified all of them. In the distance there was a dancing beam of white light – obviously the flashlight of a prison guard. Rhidian, Rebus and Red were confused. How had the guard been alerted? Was it all over? Rebus assumed, with no alarm raised that it was just an inspection. But that was going to foil everything when the guard realised that they weren't in their cells.

'Come on, move,' Rebus hissed and tugged at their sleeves. He urgently guided them across the floor. He hoped, if memory served, that there should be a set of steel steps opposite. This led to the first level of cells on the upper platform. They couldn't go up there to hide – that would definitely alert the other prisoners.

So, without saying a word, he pushed them down under the stairwell and quickly crouched in behind them. He hoped the guard wouldn't shine his torch in their direction because there wasn't much in the way of cover. They cowered down as low as they could.

'Keep quiet,' Rebus said, at barely even a whisper.

The footsteps got louder until the guard came to a stop outside the kitchen. All three prisoners held their breath. The guard only carried a *small* flashlight, which emitted a dim glow and that made Rebus smile. The prison officer pointed it at his ring of keys. He held them up in front of his eyes and selected the one he needed. Once happy with that, he slotted it into the lock and twisted – the door clicked open. Suddenly, the guard was gone. There was a hiss of relief at not being discovered.

'He's raiding the fridge,' Rebus said with a throaty chuckle. 'It's not an inspection.'

'Maybe we can slip inside the kitchen while he's in there?' Rhidian said in a hushed tone.

'No, it's too dangerous. We could easily be spotted,' Rebus grunted.

'Why didn't he put the light on inside when he went in there?' Red asked.

'Because he's not supposed to go in there. There are rules for guards too in this place. He's obviously stealing food. Anyway, the light would wake everyone up and that would be hard to explain to the warden,' Rebus answered. The guard seemed to be taking an age, but the escaping prisoners could do nothing about it.

'Come on, come on,' Rebus grumbled under his breath. 'Time is running out.' It was as if the guard had heard him and appeared again at the entrance. The small flashlight this time was under his arm, the keys were in his right hand. He was also carrying a paper bag under his other arm and was trying to juggle everything together. It was too much and he dropped the keys and stood rigid, like a shop dummy. He then gingerly waited for some reaction from the prisoners. When there was none, he stooped down to pick them up and finally slipped away down the corridor to the guardhouse.

'About time, too,' Rebus whispered. 'Come on, we've wasted enough time sitting here.' They climbed out from their hideout and moved quickly to the kitchen again. Rhidian pushed the metal skeletal key into the lock and the door just swung open.

'Wow, that was fast,' Red gushed in his ear.

'He hadn't locked it, the idiot,' Rhidian smiled back.

'Come on, inside quickly,' Rebus ordered. When they were in, he shut the door calmly and quietly behind him. He got Rhidian to lock it, just in case another guard came back and got suspicious.

'Where now?' Rhidian asked, the high pitch of his voice swirling around the cavernous room.

'Just follow my lead. Move slowly through here, the both of you. It's filled with pots and pans, as you'd expect, and if one falls in this metal room it will echo for eternity. We'll have the whole prison service in here in seconds. Got it?' They both nodded and Rebus took it for granted they'd agreed. The wizard suddenly dipped down and scurried about on the floor, like a rat looking for food.

'What are you doing?' Rhidian quizzed when he heard movement ahead.

'There's a flashlight in here somewhere. We could do with some light for the next part.' Rebus was fumbling in a cupboard and eventually found the torch.

'Won't the light give us away?' Red spoke up.

'Not this far in. We're fine, the counter and cupboards will block the light. Okay,' he announced, 'we have to get into that.' He pointed the beam to the ceiling. Small particles of dust floated around and illuminated inside the light array. There, above them, was a grid with an air vent behind it.

'That will take us out of here. The vent leads to where the heat needs to escape the building and that's where we need to climb out. There is a piece of ground outside with some trees for cover. Then it's only a small walk to the jetty and finally the sky ship.' Rhidian and Red now realised how much work the wizard had put into this whole plan and had a renewed respect for the old gent.

They climbed onto the counter and Rhidian got a knife from the cutlery drawer and unscrewed the four screws that fixed the grill to its frame. The engineer didn't release the threads completely, and left the screws still fixed on each corner (an old engineer's trick). He and Red pulled off the front cover and placed it on the worktop. They realised that any sound in the stillness of the night would project and amplify, like an explosion.

'You go up first, Rebus,' Rhidian insisted. 'You know the lay of the land. We can sort this out,' he said, pointing to the grid that had to be replaced.

Rebus climbed up with the help of the other two and quietly clambered into the squared extraction pipe, the flashlight clamped in his mouth. Then Red reached up and climbed inside after him. Rhidian gave Red the vent cover to hold so that he could climb in too. But Red fumbled it and it dropped. The square metal grid fell straight into Rhidian's grip to everyone's relief. Red's mouth was wide open – eyes bulged. Rebus shook his head and pointed the torch in Red's face. The boy looked rather sheepish.

Rhidian again handed the grid to him, but this time Red held fast. Rhidian took the cover and placed it back. Red held it in place while the engineer poked his fingers through the slots. He twisted the screws, which were still attached by only a thread. Now it looked normal and any guard that wanted a snack wouldn't notice. The three prisoners shuffled along the narrow corridor, making as little noise as possible.

They looked like three lost sheep ambling along the metal pipework. Rebus had the flashlight and Rhidian still carried the knife in case he needed to undo any more screws. There was a sound like air escaping from a balloon and Red wretched.

'Oh, Rebus, did you just fart?' Red asked, his face screwed up in disgust.

'Oops, sorry,' came the wizard's apology. 'Sprouts for lunch, I'm afraid.'

'Oh, Red,' Rhidian's voice seared from behind. 'That's disgusting.'

'It-it wasn't me,' Red said innocently. 'It was, oh, never mind.'

'It's too confined in here for that,' Rhidian complained.

'Okay, shut up you two, we're nearly there,' the old wizard declared. Rebus stopped and switched off his flashlight. There was a waft of fresh air pouring over them from the outside.

'Yes,' Rhidian gasped. Red was beaming too, as the stale air of the tube dissipated. There was a vertical, square vent cover ahead.

'Red, give me a hand with this. We don't want to make any noise, usual drill,' Rebus instructed.

'I know, Rebus, you've told me a thousand times,' Red bit back, fed up of being constantly reminded.

'Hey, a little respect,' Rhidian scolded from behind. 'He's only saying.'

'Sorry, Rebus. I guess I'm a bit agitated,' Red apologised. Rebus then switched off the torch.

'No problem, young fella, we're all a bit scared,' the wizard agreed. 'Right, let's lift this off.' But it was fixed on the bottom and when they pushed away from its fixings, it fell out of their hands and slapped down on the wall outside. The bottom hinges held it in place, but it made a short clanging noise when it hit the brick surface and everyone stopped. Rebus was waiting for the

73

fallout, but after a minute of waiting there was no movement below or inside.

'Phew, that was too close,' Rebus gasped. 'Come on, we have to climb down to the ground quickly.'

There was a full moon, which was not in their favour. A full moon was brighter up in the clouds where the prison was situated. Rebus could clearly see the outline of the prison perimeter and the jetty was lit up. Just beyond the jetty were the sparkly lights of the sky ships – there were two. One preparing to leave and the other would be moving off in the morning.

They had to make sure no one saw them crawling down the wall. The drop to the bottom was only a matter of two metres or so.

Rebus awkwardly clambered out and climbed down the grid. Once he was at the end of the frame, he let go. He landed with a light thud.

It was Red's turn next and he did the same. Shortly after, Rhidian joined them. There was no way of closing the vent cover, so they had to leave it open. Hopefully they would be far away from here before anyone noticed.

They ducked into the tree line and hid amongst the shadows. It was only a matter of moving from their position and slipping past the guard on the jetty. Then they would be home free.

The only problem was that there were two guards tonight and that was going to be a more difficult task. Rhidian looked at Rebus. Rebus gravely looked at the two of them and shrugged his shoulders. How were they to get past these two?

Chapter 6
Sky Ship

The three darkened figures – Rebus the wizard, Rhidian and Red – moved as quietly as they could through the trees and tried as they might to keep under cover.

'I don't like this, Rebus. We're totally exposed out here,' Rhidian shrieked breathlessly as he ran along the open ground. The moon was big and full and totally wasn't helping in the "hide and seek" operation. When the cover became so sparse, they had to duck down and scurry along a shabby line of bushes, which was perched on the very crest of the jetty.

'We all here?' Rebus whispered. 'Red?'

'Yeah, I'm right here,' the boy responded. Rebus could see Rhidian as he popped his head over the edge of the bushes, only enough so that the enemy couldn't see him.

'What can you see, Rhidian?' Rebus mumbled, trying to push up and look for himself. Rhidian restrained him by pushing his head back down.

'Stay down,' he hissed. 'There are definitely only two guards on the pier,' Rhidian observed.

'How are we going to get past them without giving ourselves away? There's only one route,' he said, his mouth barely open when he spoke. He squinted and looked beyond the guards at the two ships that waited for them. So near, Rhidian thought. A sinking feeling filled the pit of his stomach. Time was running out. The three of them realised that at some point, someone would notice that their cells were empty. How much time did they have left?

'Don't tell me we're stuck here?' Red sounded scared. The fear of being forced back to that cell made him feel ill. He was almost in tears. 'I didn't come all this way to go back. I'm not going back.' He was determined. He was losing it and someone had to do something. Rebus reached out and grabbed his arm.

'Oi, get a grip, boy. If it wasn't for me you'd be stuck in your cell right now,' Rebus snarled. 'I never said things would be easy, did I? We just have to find a way out of this situation,' he continued on a more positive note. Red was taken aback.

'S-sorry, Rebus,' Red apologised, realising how right the wizard was.

'Keep quiet, the both of you, or we'll be caught for sure,' Rhidian snapped.

They did indeed have a huge problem and a plan had to be formulated and fast. It wouldn't be long before the first ship would be ready to take sail.

'What time do you reckon it is?' Red asked. Rebus held his hand to the moon and half covered it with his fingers.

'It's about eight forty-seven,' Rebus answered. Rhidian and Red looked really impressed.

'Wow, how on earth do you know that, old man?' Rhidian pressed. 'Wizard's magic?'

'No,' Rebus said, and produced a pocket watch from his pouch. 'I just looked at this,' he said with a smirk. The engineer and Red rolled their eyes – they'd been duped. Rhidian turned to look at the jetty again.

'That means we have just about forty minutes to get past the guards, board, and make a clean getaway,' Rhidian said with a hint of despair. 'Sounds easy,' he said sarcastically.

'That's right, so let's get on with it,' Rebus insisted.

The two sky ships were nestled in the bay. Both were tethered to each side of the long, sweeping jetty. There was one with its zeppelin-type balloon floating high above. It was the ship that had brought Rhidian there, and the other carrying the airbag below.

At the centre was a bench with two prison guards. They were just chatting to one another rather than guarding the ships. No one had ever attempted to climb aboard a ship, so they weren't overly concerned.

Twilight bathed the whole scene in a whitish glow, making it impossible for the three prisoners to sneak past without being detected.

'We'll be seen straight away as soon as we step out. The moon is like a searchlight out there,' Rhidian grimaced. 'Crap,' he cursed. He had one last look and then slipped back down with his colleagues and huffed.

'There's got to be another way,' Rebus said, a real concern in his voice. 'We do have one thing going for us.' There was silence for a moment.

'And what's that, Rebus?' Rhidian said with folded arms.

'The element of surprise,' he said with confidence. 'They won't be expecting us, and that's our saviour.'

'But that's not going to make much difference,' Red said. 'There's only one way across, surprise or not. I don't mean to be negative, but it does seem hopeless.'

'Oh shut up, boy. If you can't think of anything positive to say, say nothing at all,' Rebus scolded. He rubbed his chin and thought as hard as he could, looking for an answer.

'What if we cause a distraction?' Rhidian said, as his eyes rolled around, grasping for an idea to help them. 'Then when they go to investigate, we can slip on board. Would that work?'

'No, that won't work, Rhidian,' Rebus was adamant.

'Why not?' Rhidian looked wounded.

'Because only one will investigate. They're not stupid,' the wizard said and shook his head. 'And if we try to take the other one, that could cause a huge commotion and we don't want that. No, we have to think of something else. This is the last obstacle and we can't fail now.'

'What do we do then?' Red chirped up again.

'Well, let's think about this.' Rebus weighed up the situation. 'We'll be seen if we simply walk up to them. There's no other way to slip past them either. We can't distract them.' Rebus was beginning to look as dismayed as the others.

'We can't approach them dressed in these orange boiler suits. They'll see we're inmates for sure,' Rhidian said and puffed out a mouthful of air.

'Really, we need to be ghosts...' Rebus stopped talking for a moment and then his eyes lit as if he'd been given the keys to a world of wealth. 'That's it,' he exclaimed joyfully.

'That's what?' Rhidian asked.

'Yeah, what have you come up with, Rebus?' Red added, sounding impatient.

'It's a long shot, but we haven't much time for anything else,' he mumbled.

'What's a long shot? You're not making much sense, man.' Rhidian hated being kept in the dark.

'Hold on a sec. Let me try something first,' Rebus added. Rhidian and Red looked on with wild curiosity. Rebus sat down and pressed his index fingers to his temples and closed his eyes. He meditated for a minute or so with a stern look of concentration on his face. The tightness of his facial expression soon relaxed and was replaced with a broad smile. The wizard opened his eyes and sat looking completely smug.

'What?' Rhidian uttered, getting to the point of boiling over.

'Yeah, come on, Rebus, don't keep us in suspense,' Red said, hoping there was a way out of this.

'Get up,' he said and stood in full view of the enemy. Rhidian tried to grab at Rebus' sleeve, but the old wizard swiped off the advance.

'What are you doing? Are you mad?' Rhidian rasped in anger. 'You're jeopardising our whole escape – get back down here.' But Rebus stood his ground.

'Just trust me. Get up,' Rebus repeated and looked calm. Rhidian looked at Red and shrugged his shoulders. The engineer had noticed one thing though: either the guards hadn't seen the wizard standing up, or maybe he hadn't been seen because something else had taken place. The two reluctantly stood up next to the wizard, cringing, waiting to be spotted.

'What are we doing, Rebus?' Rhidian felt so exposed out here as he followed the wizard onto the jetty.

Red reluctantly dragged himself after them. What am I doing? the boy thought. He couldn't believe this was happening. He felt his heart beat loudly in his chest.

'Are we just going to walk up to them?' Rhidian squeaked through thin lips.

'Just follow my lead,' Rebus said, sounding really uninhibited.

Red kept quiet in the background. He hid behind the two men, as if concealing himself behind them would make any difference.

Rhidian walked tentatively along the wooden jetty and noticed something odd. They were halfway along and the guards hadn't challenged them yet. He peered at Rebus in wonderment. The jetty moved slightly underfoot, as a cool breeze wafted over them. They literally felt as if they were walking on air.

'This is weird,' Rhidian said, feeling a little more confident too. Why hadn't they been spotted yet? Something was going on.

'Keep going, Rhidian, there's a good fellow,' Rebus instructed, not taking his eyes from the guards. Rhidian turned back towards Red and nodded. The boy acknowledged, but his face was tight with fear.

The trio had made it three quarters of the way, and could almost see the eyes of the guards in the half-light. If it hadn't been for the fact that they were escaping convicts, it would seem as though they were only taking an evening stroll in the moonlight. Red darted his eyes around like a manic chicken.

'What are they doing?' Red piped up from behind. 'I thought we would have been escorted back to our cells by now.'

'Keep quiet, boy, and just follow me. We may just get away with this yet,' Rebus hissed in an intense whisper.

Red stopped talking and continued to follow on wobbly legs – his nerves had really got the better of him. Whatever Rebus had formulated seemed to be working. They were almost there and, suddenly, as the three fugitives approached, one of the guards stepped forward. They all stopped and held their breath. There was a momentary lapse in time, where everything appeared still. One of the guards broke the silence.

'Is it that time already?' he uttered, looking directly at Rebus.

Rhidian was gobsmacked. Here they were, three prisoners in orange prison-issue boiler suits and the guards were treating them as the changeover shift. Whatever Rebus had done was definitely working.

'Yes, we've come to relieve you fine gentlemen,' Rebus said with such sickly charm that would make a turtle dove throw up. Rhidian had to stifle a snort.

'Fine by us,' said the second man. 'I'm starving. Come on, George, it's stew night.' The two prison guards stood up and stretched.

'Yes, you go and enjoy your meal and rest up,' Rebus added.

'Enjoy your shift, lads,' one said with a snigger.

'Yeah, nighty-night,' the other joked and then the two officers didn't ask any more questions and walked off contentedly. They had no idea that they were indeed letting three prisoners escape. Rhidian watched them step off the jetty and turned to Rebus. All three of them let out a huge sigh, trying not to laugh.

'You crafty devil,' Rhidian said. 'How did you know that the magic had returned? In fact, how has your magic come back?'

'The answer to that is simple – it hasn't,' Rebus assured him. 'It was a chance I had to take – it's mind control, not magic. It would either work or we would have been discovered,' he said.

'A chance? So it could have all gone terribly wrong? Well I'm glad it did work,' Red remarked with a sigh.

'There was no other way. Come on, there's no time to lose chitchatting. We need to take one of these ships and get out of here as soon as possible. They are bound to find out soon and I would like to be many miles away by then,' Rebus confessed.

'Yeah, me too, Rebus, but which one?' Rhidian asked. 'Won't they have a small crew on board?' he added.

'No, I'm hoping that both crews are in the civilian canteen back there,' he said, and pointed to one of the darkened buildings in the distance. 'That's why they have guards – to make sure no one boards the empty ships while they're eating. This one should be ready to sail,' Rebus said, and indicated one of the craft. He'd researched this in great detail. It was the one without the balloon thankfully. Rhidian was relieved.

'How do you know that?' Red asked.

'Everything is tied down, lad.'

Rhidian then realised why Rebus had chosen it. 'I've seen this a million times. I guess you have *too,* Rebus? If everything is secured then a ship is ready for its voyage.' Rebus nodded in agreement. In fact, seeing the ships coming and going was all he'd been focussed on since being trapped on the rock.

'Let's take it then and get out of here,' Rhidian said, and made his way to the ship Rebus had chosen. 'If we untether it, it will drift off without any noise and once we're out of earshot, we can start her up.'

'Sounds good to me,' Rebus agreed, and so did Red for once.

Chapter 7
Voyage

'OK, let's get on board, but quietly,' Rebus whispered. 'We'd better be careful and check to make sure there's no crewmen left, just in case.' Rebus didn't want to be too confident and compromise their escape. They'd only need one person to sound the alarm and the whole escape would be fruitless, and probably their last chance to break free from Skytraz Prison.

'Quietly, Red, follow Rebus and I and don't make any sudden movements,' Rhidian insisted, as he steadily walked up the gangplank.

The wooden board dipped slightly with their weight, just as if the ship were moored on the sea. The air was cool and still and only the fleeting sound of a gull ripped the silence. Rebus, Rhidian and Red climbed onto the deck. The worn timbers groaned and creaked, like an old sailor complaining about the weather.

The vessel was a medium-sized supply ship and Rhidian was fairly sure he could pilot it. He'd worked on similar ships in the past – being an engineer he had to be versatile.

The three of them stealthy searched the cabins for any signs of life. Time was ticking away and every moment counted. They regrouped on the deck after finding no crew on board. There was a sigh of relief from all concerned.

Rhidian disappeared for a minute or so and left their ship and climbed on board the second ship. Rebus looked on in puzzlement; he grimaced.

'What's he doing?' Rebus quizzed Red. 'We haven't time to mess about – we have to get out of here.' He was annoyed, his eyes filled with fire.

'He said it was to make sure there was no one on that ship too. So they wouldn't alert the others.' Red relayed what Rhidian had told him. Rebus said nothing to this, but peered into the shadows of the sister vessel. He raked his fingers through his well-groomed beard and appeared tense.

'He wouldn't have gone if it wasn't important, Rebus, I'm sure of it,' Red said in Rhidian's defence. Rebus admired Red for his loyalty; the boy's learning, he thought. A few gruelling minutes ticked by and eventually there was movement on the deck of the other ship.

'You took your time. What are you up to?' Rebus commented.

'Just an insurance policy,' Rhidian said, and no more.

Rhidian then asked Red to give him a hand to unhitch the ropes from their moorings. The boy shimmied down the gangplank and met the engineer. The two of them tossed the ropes to Rebus for him to secure and he coiled them in a spool on the deck. The two then ran up the gangplank and, once they pulled it in, they were ready to leave.

The ship began to ease away from the jetty, drifting into the open sky. The tension in Red's stomach began to ease but this wasn't over yet. Rhidian told the others to keep a lookout for any signs of frantic activity, just in case they'd been found out. He then dashed to the navigation room. He steered the ship away from Skytraz Prison and slowly drifted out of dock.

Red stood rigid as a statue, watching the rock prison slowly get smaller and smaller. Rebus didn't speak for a while, either; this was a very scary time. The darkness was good camouflage. Red kept his eyes peeled, licking his lips and breathing shallow.

Being an engineer, Rhidian knew that Sky Ships worked in a similar way to a hot air balloon, but with the added propulsion of an engine. Most of the ships had cushioned airbags, whilst older models (like the one he'd arrived on, moored opposite) still held zeppelin-type balloons above. The giant airbags on this freighter fitted along the whole length and width of the vessel's underside.

It had everything ingeniously weighted to keep the air-borne ship from capsizing.

He remembered reading up on Professor Jenk's invention, the pioneer of the "floating base". This made it possible to have the balloon underneath and not above the ship – a great step forward, making the balloon skin easier to protect. The old zeppelin-type vessels were vulnerable to attack. The hot air balloons would be the main targets. Their highly inflammable gas would explode if the material used for the balloon was punctured by pirates or rogue fire.

These days they used a non-flammable liquid and a thick outer skin. And with the balloon fitted to the underside, there was almost no chance of puncture and any danger of explosion. Rhidian detracted from his engineering lesson and called back to the others.

'How are we doing? Are we far enough away yet?' he hissed as he stuck his head out of the cabin.

'Just a little further, my friend, and you can start the engine,' Rebus called back.

'It still looks quiet. There's no movement from what I can make out, Rhidian,' Red's voice cut across the deck.

'Okay, but we have to get away as quickly as we can,' he relayed as quietly as he could. Within a couple of minutes, Rebus joined him in the control room. They waited until it was just the right time and when they thought they were out of earshot, Rebus spoke.

'All right, Rhidian,' he said in his full voice. 'Start her up.' Rhidian then primed the engine with a few pumps of a plunger. Once he was satisfied it was enough, he then pressed the button to start the engine. It seemed to turn over but coughed and spluttered as if it was getting over a cold. Rebus gritted his teeth in frustration and hoped the engine sound hadn't travelled back to the prison.

'What's the problem, Rhidian?' Rebus asked, and looked concerned, his face white. 'We have to get out of here now. Can you pilot this thing or not?' he rasped.

'Hold on a second, Rebus. I'm a little rusty and this engine has been lazing all day. Just give me a moment, will you?' he grunted, just as frustrated as the wizard. 'I don't want to over prime her. Once she's flooded then we'll have real problems.' Rebus stood back, not knowing anything about the combustion engine and let Rhidian get on with it. As a wizard you have to understand things before you can use any magic and the enormity of the ship would take all his magical strength. He may need that for later.

The next moment, Red came flying into the control room and looked really concerned.

'I-I th-think they've found out we've gone,' he bellowed.

'How do you know? What did you see, boy?' Rebus pressed.

'Come see for yourself.' Red led Rebus outside. Sure enough, when Rebus looked far into the distance, he could see glittering lights of many flashlights and a siren echoed through the air, alerting the whole prison.

'RHIDIAN... WE NEED TO GO NOW!' Rebus boomed.

'I know, I know,' Rhidian winced. His hands were clammy and sweat was dripping from his brow onto the dials of the console. He'd run every scenario he could think of, but he knew that under pressure he could and would make mistakes. He stood back – why wasn't it starting? He again ran all the procedure through his mind – every sequence, every scenario. Pump the fuel to prime the engine... press the start button and... He scratched his head.

'RHIDIAN!' Even Red was joining in on the chorus now. Rhidian had both hands on his mouth, breathing through his fingers. He swallowed hard and panted furiously. This is basic, basic engineering, he scolded himself. Why isn't the fuel...? He stopped; something came to him.

'Hold on,' he said. 'I've primed the engine and pressed the start button.' He smacked his forehead with the heel of his hand. 'How stupid of me,' he muttered. 'I haven't flicked on the petrol feed – basic engineering. Of course, the engine is starved of fuel.'

'RHIDIAN, now would be a good time!' Rebus screamed from the deck. Rhidian once again pumped the plunger and then he flicked the switch. When that was done he crossed his fingers for a moment... and then pressed the start-up button. The engine coughed, spluttered and exploded into life. The jolt from the propeller shook the ship. Rhidian grabbed the power lever and eased it forward. The ship began to pick up speed; it wasn't only the wind moving it now – the power of the engine was in full thrust. He could hear the howls and hoots of delight from the old wizard and the boy. He rested his clammy hands on the steering console. They'd done it. They'd escaped from Skytraz. But it wasn't time to celebrate yet; they had to make sure they were far enough away first.

Rebus came bursting into the control room, his face reddened by the rush. Red was two steps behind him.

'Come on, man, get this ship out of here fast,' he demanded.

'We're at full thrust. Why, what's the problem?' Rhidian answered back.

'They've got that second ship and they'll soon be on our tail,' Rebus said, and looked more flustered than Rhidian had ever seen him.

'They won't catch us now,' Rhidian said confidently.

'How do you know that?' Red responded. 'That other ship could be faster than this one.'

'It doesn't matter how fast it is,' Rhidian said with a smile. 'It won't start without this,' he said, holding out a short piece of electrical flex.

'What's that?' Rebus asked curiously.

'It's the main starter motor lead. Without it, the engine won't start up,' he answered smugly.

'You crafty dog,' Rebus giggled. In fact, all three of them danced a jig around the control room, laughing and cheering as they did so.

The ship glided through the sky, riding the air as calm as a bird. Before long, it was a small dot in the distance and then it disappeared completely.

Chapter 8
Hope

Mia rubbed at the wooden table with her soft polishing cloth in a half-hearted attempt at getting it to shine. To be fair it was already polished to a high standard, but Jenta-Lor expected everything to be in pristine condition. She adjusted the stiff collar on her blouse and yanked it away from her throat. She sighed and swirled the cloth in circles, not really thinking of the job at all. She hated it here.

Since she had been taken, totally against her will, and forced to work in this place, she had no enthusiasm for the work. But at least she wasn't thrown into prison, or maybe worse, but her mind was on other things. There wasn't a minute that went by that she hadn't thought about Rhidian. A knot tugged at her stomach. She hadn't been told anything and wanted to ask on many occasions, but kept quiet.

Was he all right? What was he doing? Was he thinking of her too? Was he being harmed? Her stomach tightened again at the last thought as she looked at her reflection in the wood.

Her pretty face had lost its sparkle. A dulled, sad reflection vacantly stared back from the mahogany surface. She noticed dark circles under her eyes and knew it was because of the sleepless nights. Her forehead now carried worry lines in place of her previous smooth skin. She blinked back a tear that pushed at the corner of her eye and the sadness gripped her throat. She tried to settle and tried to think of happier times; it was difficult. She needed to know something about her husband. Stop being so soft, she told herself as she straightened her shoulders.

Mia moved from surface to surface, doing exactly the same job as she'd done the day before. She came across the one door that she wasn't allowed to enter. She thought it strange that she had access to all other rooms in this place, other than this one. She could even clean and polish in Jenta-Lor's study, under supervision, of course. They didn't want her seeing any information that didn't concern her. But this door was totally "out of bounds" and she wasn't even allowed to go in there with a chaperone. What was so important in there that she wasn't permitted to see? This always intrigued her. She stood for a moment, pondering, and felt a slight tickle deep in her gut.

She soon snapped out of her thoughts when she heard raised voices from Jenta-Lor's study. This was strange; she realised something was up.

The house had been really quiet. She hadn't been there long, but presumed that this was the general atmosphere. That was the only godsend of being trapped, the tranquillity.

The staff had put her to work straight away and as long as she got on with it, they left her alone. She was alone now, but the heightened tone of the conversation was intriguing. She found herself needing to investigate.

There were only the two dividing doors that separated the study from the waiting room where she was working. That seemed to be where the commotion was coming from. Mia wondered if she could listen without the other servants or Jenta-Lor's main staff catching her. She needed to keep her head down or she didn't know where they would put her next.

Mia casually walked from the centre table and polished her way to the study entrance. Each side of the big doors were two smaller tables, with a vase on each one – that was her opportunity. If I polish those now, it won't look as though I'm spying, she thought. She placed her cloth on the side and lifted the vase off the stand. She'd remembered that Jenta-Lor's desk was situated to the left side of the study, that's why she chose the left table to polish.

The vase itself was quite heavy too and at one stage almost slipped from her grasp. Her stomach knotted and she opened her mouth in shock, eyes bulging. Mia then gently placed it on the floor, next to the table, and let out a shallow sigh. Then she retrieved her polishing cloth and leaned forward and pressed her right ear to the door. She pretended to polish and listened at the same time, making sure to look around for anyone who might catch her.

The conversation was a bit muffled at first, so she had to strain to hear it correctly. She squinted in concentration. She then felt someone approach and eased back from the door, looked down onto the table surface and continued polishing. A tall servant swept past and didn't even acknowledge she was there.

She watched as he walked down the corridor and disappeared into another room. She let out a huge breath of air. That was too close, she thought. She again checked to see if anyone was watching; there wasn't. Mia quickly pressed her ear against the cold surface of the door once more and this time closed her eyes and focussed.

'What did you say?' She heard one voice growl angrily. It sounded like Jenta-Lor himself. The other voice was meek under Jenta-Lor's overbearing tone.

'M-y lord,' the voice stammered, 'the report has just come in to say prisoners have esc-aped.'

'What are those buffoons doing over there in Skytraz Prison? You are supposed to be running a jail that is inescapable – how could they let this happen?' Jenta-Lor bellowed.

'They're on lock-down now, my lord, so that no one else can escape,' the other voice grovelled.

'It's a little bit late for that now, isn't it?' Jenta-Lor screamed, 'I don't know why you don't let them all escape,' he said, the sarcasm oozing from every pore. 'Do we have the numbers and names of the prisoners that got away, or has the paperwork escaped too?' Jenta-Lor continued to mock.

'Yes, my lord, I have the names here.' Mia thought she heard someone step forward and maybe a piece of paper being ruffled.

There was another sound of echoed footsteps that scurried down the hall. Mia had to quickly look as though she was cleaning again. She cursed herself that she'd miss the names of the escaped prisoners. One of the kitchen staff shuffled past her and scurried away. Mia waited for only a second and didn't waste any more time. She planted her ear against the door again like a suction cup, hoping she hadn't missed any vital information. But she needn't have worried.

'Rhidian Fines and Rebus!' Jenta-Lor screamed.

'And Red, a young boy...' the officer didn't have time to finish.

'I don't care about any boy, you idiot. How could this happen? How did they escape?' Jenta-Lor continued his rant.

A huge smile filled Mia's face and her heart was beating much faster now at the news. He *was* in Skytraz Prison, she'd gathered as much. She didn't care for the details of the escape, only that he was out and free. She stepped away from the door and put the vase back in place.

'He's escaped, he's escaped,' she repeated, trying to keep her voice to a whisper, almost jumping up and down on the spot. This fresh information lifted her spirits and made things a little easier to manage, knowing he was at least safe for now.

She moved away from the door and busied herself with the other furniture in the room, when suddenly the doors to the study burst open. She turned with a start. Jenta-Lor walked across the waiting room in a fast-paced march – the officer scrambled behind. He looked at Mia and stopped. He stood and gave a long penetrating glare.

'You know, don't you?' he questioned, his eyes like lasers.

'I'm sorry, my lord, know what?' she lied, keeping her refrain from slipping into a grin. He peered in her eyes, searching for the truth.

'You know that, err, never mind,' he growled, dismissing her and continued on down the corridor.

The officer shadowing him gave her a sweeping stern glance as he swept past. She heard the slam of a door and they were gone. For the first time in all the commotion of the last couple of days she felt good. Get back to me somehow, my love, she pondered lovingly, and soon.

Chapter 9
The Stowaway

'Where are we headed?' Rhidian enquired as he stared through the window into the steely skies. The grey wisps of cloud were thinning to reveal the early beginnings of a new morning. The ship chugged along at a steady pace. Rhidian stood at the wheel, feeling a little tired.

'We have to get as much distance between us and Skytraz Prison as possible,' Rebus announced, and scratched his perfectly trimmed beard. Rhidian turned and looked directly at Red. He was standing quietly in the corner, listening and taking in the conversation without commenting. Rhidian smiled at the teenager and Red gave a polite grin back.

'You're quiet for a change,' Rhidian said. 'Anything wrong?'

'I'm fine,' the boy reacted in a whisper, having to clear his throat. He hadn't spoken for a while and his mouth was dry. 'It's just…' He paused. Rebus and Rhidian looked at him.

'What?' Rhidian enquired squinting in curiosity. 'What's the matter? you can tell us.'

'I'm… hungry,' he said simply, 'and I didn't want to bring it up.'

It was quite amusing to the engineer, the idea of the boy being hungry. Especially after their traumatic escape from the prison. They'd broken out of their cells. They'd made it to the ship, whilst fooling the prison guards in the process. All that taking place, excitement and fear, and now – the boy was hungry! Rhidian chuckled to himself. He'd been a teenager once too, and food could be more important to a kid than anything.

'Why don't you make yourself useful and see if there's anything on board. We could all do with something to eat I suppose,' Rhidian expressed, flicking his gaze to the old wizard. 'I know I'm hungry too – steak would be nice.' The thought made his stomach rumble.

'Yes, I could use a bite,' Rebus added. 'There must be something in the galley, boy. Have a good look around. The kitchen must have food for the crew.'

'Yeah, okay,' Red agreed, and perked up a notch when he thought of all the possible food there might be. 'I'll find something.' He hurriedly turned around and made his way out of the control room. He was more than ready to search and see what treasures were in the kitchen.

'Do you want me to come with you?' Rebus called out after him. 'You may need help.'

'No, I'll be fine, old man,' the teenager replied, his voice fading with the wind as he disappeared onto the deck. Rhidian almost burst out laughing but managed to hold it in.

'Old man, indeed,' Rebus grumbled, rolling his tongue around in his mouth. 'Cheeky young scamp,' he moaned, grinding his teeth.

Red stopped halfway along the deck. He closed his eyes for a moment and drank in the cool early morning breeze. Right now it was the best feeling in the world. He was free of that awful prison and that was a relief in itself. He opened his eyes again and walked purposely across the ship's decking – his stomach tickled with the pitch and roll of its camber. The woodwork groaned and Red's stomach grumbled along in sympathy, reminding him of his purpose: food!

He looked down at his orange boiler suit, a stabbing reminder of his brief time spent locked up. He shook his head and told himself that he wasn't going back there, ever! He'd done nothing wrong anyway and thought of his arrest.

The Jenta Police came and, without any explanation, took him away. What had he done that was so bad to send him to Skytraz Prison of all places? He broke away from his thoughts and took a deep breath.

'Okay, where is the food kept?' he wondered.

The dawn would have been enough to guide him, but there were enough lights speckled around the deck and along the inner buildings. Red didn't know a lot about sky ships; he didn't really need to. He'd only known about the comings and goings of the city since he'd been born.

He'd watched the ships though, on many occasions, delivering supplies and then disappearing across the sky to another city. He never thought he'd actually be on one, one day.

He loved Valusha and never intended to leave; why would he? He'd made friends there and thought that would be his life. His stomach groaned again and he pushed all other thoughts to one side.

'Where would the galley be?' he mumbled. He wandered aimlessly without any idea of where the kitchen was situated on a ship. He did eventually find a small door, turned the handle and pushed it open to reveal a set of steps. There were lights above that shone a beam to the bottom, but it looked a bit dark beyond. Rhidian had checked this area earlier, looking for stray crewmen, and now Red realised that he had to go down alone. He cleared his throat, which echoed a warning.

'Come on, Red, you're a man, for God's sake,' he reassured himself.

The wooden stairway took the boy down into the bowels of the ship. To his utter surprise, it also took him to the kitchen. There was another door, and once he stepped inside, he saw an oven and a greedy grin engulfed his face. He could feel the saliva rise in his mouth.

There was only minimal lighting down here and he didn't even care at this point – food was his only goal. The teenager didn't waste any time and moved along in the dimness of the room. He urgently began searching the cupboards. He delved into the stainless steel units, banging and clattering as he searched. The look of distaste consumed him when he only found pots, pans and cutlery. He clenched his teeth and grunted, childishly tossing a frying pan along the floor. It came to a stop with a clatter.

'Where is the food?' he demanded. His voice echoed in the empty cylinder of the galley. He urgently looked beyond the cupboards and noticed there was another door. It's got to be in there, he assumed. His mood worsened and the groans in his stomach turned to stabbing hunger pains. He hurriedly shuffled to the back of the kitchen. There on the door was a plaque with the title "Food Store" written in big letters. A bright smile brightened his mood.

'Yes.' He felt himself punching the air. The boy eagerly twisted the handle and pushed it open, excitement spilling over. Inside were shelves with tins and packets lined up along the inside walls. Red urgently scoured the room and to one side he noticed a freezer and a FRIDGE!

The soft orange glow of the lighting in the pantry reflected in the stainless-steel panelling. He'd made it. He didn't need any more encouragement and went directly for the cold food cabinet. He threw open the door and the white light hurt his eyes for a moment. It was only temporary though, and he soon focused on the full-to-bursting shelves. The brilliance of the inside lit his pale face. There was an array of cold meats and cheeses, pastries and desserts, drinks and fruit. The aroma of cooked ham and orange juice overwhelmed his nostrils. The saliva almost dripped from his mouth and he had to swallow back not to dribble over his boiler suit. He was just about to pounce!

'Don't move, kid!' The deep gravelled voice of a man bore into the back of his head. Red almost choked, his body stiffened, mouth dropped open – his breath came in sharp bursts and the loud pounding of his heart impaired his hearing. He was physically shaking.

'Wha…' he couldn't speak. Then he felt something jab in between his shoulder blades – he let out a short gasp.

'Don't try anything stupid.' The voice came again, harsh and low. 'Who are you, kid? What are you doing here?' Red didn't know what to say; he was stunned.

'I-I…' But it was impossible for him to speak. The revelation of a knife penetrating his skin terrified him. I'm going to die right now, he thought, and tears welled up.

'Come on back from there,' the man demanded, and pulled at his collar. Red was jerked away from the treasure trove of foodstuff. He was too scared to even think of his stomach any more. He trembled and felt that his legs wouldn't hold his body weight.

'Ok-ay,' he stuttered, trying to catch his breath. The boy stood with the man still behind him, terrified to turn and face whatever was coming. The door to the fridge left open and the stupidest feeling of shutting it gripped him. He'd always been told to keep the cold air in, but that was the least of his worries. Red took a deep breath and plucked up the courage and spoke.

'P-lease don't kill me,' he pleaded and tried to catch his breath as he sobbed. 'I haven't done anything wrong.'

'Leave him be.' Another voice filled the room and Red recognised it straight away as being that of Rebus. All of a sudden a huge sigh of hope lifted his spirits, but this was far from over. Red felt the intruder physically shake. Was he scared too? 'And take that spoon from away from the kid's back,' Rebus added.

'SPOON?' Red's reaction changed from frightened to downright annoyed. 'SPOON?' he repeated. 'You've been threatening me with a spoon?' He spat the word as if it were a bad taste in his mouth. He spun around to face his attacker and came face to face with a meek-looking middle-aged man. He stood roughly five foot nine and quite thin. Red was mesmerised by his steel-blue eyes. He also had a scar on his left cheek, which was in the shape of a half-moon and it was quite a prominent feature.

'Who are you?' Rebus questioned abruptly, his eyes not deviating from the stranger's look of dismay.

'I-I…' It was the stranger's turn now to fumble his words. He didn't have the husky gravelled voice that he'd put on earlier. 'I'm Caleb,' he finally answered, as if he'd been introduced at a party.

'What are you doing here?' Red butted in, but Rebus raised his left hand in an attempt to stop the youngster talking. 'I'll deal with this, shh,' he said sternly, putting his finger to his lips.

'What *are* you doing here?' Rebus probed asking exactly the same question. Caleb placed the dessertspoon on the nearest shelf and sighed.

'I'm a stowaway,' he admitted. 'I've been hidden away on here for a week or so.' He raised his hands and gestured where he'd stayed.

'Why?' Rebus continued, before Red could open his mouth to speak again.

'Things were getting bad on Valusha and I had to get away,' he spoke honestly. 'I stowed away on here thinking it would take me to somewhere to start a new life. But I didn't get away immediately; they'd delivered supplies on Valusha and the crew took some time off. Then eventually they boarded again, but had one more stop and went onto Skytraz Prison. That scared me. I didn't want to end up there, so I kept hidden as the crew off-loaded supplies. This particular ship was then, I hoped, going onto somewhere where I could get off and disappear. But, that's when I heard voices. They didn't sound like the usual voices of the crew and there were only a couple of you, I presumed. I didn't know what to do. I realised that you were escaped prisoners when I saw the orange boiler suits. I panicked when the boy came into the kitchen. I apologise for that, boy,' he said.

Rebus looked deep into his eyes; he seemed genuine enough. Why would he be hidden on this ship otherwise? He would have raised the alarm straightaway if he'd been one of the crew.

'Okay, let's go see Rhidian,' Rebus announced. 'Come on.' He pointed to the exit.

110

'Who's Rhidian? How did you manage to get past the guards? Where are we headed?' Caleb was full of questions.

'Don't you worry about that. That's our business,' Red chipped in, not being able to keep quiet and trying to sound older than his years. He got a stern look from Rebus, but that was all.

'Food,' Red uttered, side-tracking the comment. 'There's plenty of food in here,' he said, pointing to the open fridge. Again, his eyes lit up at the array of delicious things on display.

'Good, grab a bit of everything and let's go,' Rebus instructed. He waited for Red to put a few things in a canvas bag that he found hanging behind the door. When it was full, all three walked out of the galley, up the stairway and onto the deck. It was almost full daylight now and they could see the stranger in all his glory.

Rebus kept a sharp eye, suspicious to the last.

'You go in front so that we can keep an eye on you. Make your way to the control room. Rhidian is there,' Rebus remarked. Red followed behind Rebus, chewing a mouthful of meat, not being able to wait any longer.

Chapter 10
Team Hope

They all gathered in the control room.

'Who's this?' Rhidian said, and he looked deeply curious and surprised to see an extra person on board.

'This is Caleb,' Rebus announced. 'He's been a stowaway on here, apparently. He's escaped Valusha and is trying to find safety.' Rhidian eyed the stranger, still not totally convinced by his story.

'You believe him?' Rhidian gave a concerned look at Rebus.

'I am in the room, you know,' Caleb interrupted, feeling a little hurt.

'Well, why would he lie?' Rebus said, slightly siding with the stranger – Caleb looked surprised. 'I mean,' Rebus continued, 'he could have raised the alarm at any time, couldn't he? But he didn't. And he didn't know anything of our attempt beforehand either… to be a spy, I mean, and report it back to someone.' Rhidian considered this for a moment, then his face lit up.

'Great, we could do with some extra help on this trip,' he said.

'I don't trust him,' Red cut in sharply. 'He jumped me in the kitchen and used a, uh, err, weapon to attack me.' Rhidian arched his eyebrow and peered back at the youngster.

'You don't trust me, kid? I understand that, but the weapon—' Caleb attempted to go on, but was interrupted by the irate teenager.

'You tried to stab me,' Red added quickly, 'and I'm not a kid. My name is Red.'

'A *spoon*, Red. He attacked you with a spoon!' Rebus corrected.

'A spoon, eh?' Rhidian said, smiling. 'He certainly is a dangerous customer.'

'It's not funny, Rhidian.' Red was getting annoyed. 'He could have killed me.'

'I do apologise, young man,' Caleb relented. 'It would have taken me a while to spoon you to death though.' This made Red even angrier and his embarrassment showed in the pink tinges in his cheeks. Rhidian could see that the boy was getting too agitated and pulled the conversation on a different heading.

'What have you got in your hand, Red?' Rhidian asked; he'd noticed the bag he was holding.

'Oh, it's food. I picked a load of stuff from the fridge,' Red said, and for a moment lost track of the conversation.

'Well, let's all have some food and drink and discuss where we're headed,' Rhidian announced.

'Makes sense to me,' Rebus added and Caleb nodded in agreement.

'Oh, okay.' Red suddenly remembered how hungry he was. All four of them sat, as there was a couple of chairs and a counter in the control room. Red emptied his bag of goodies for all to tuck in.

'It wouldn't be a bad idea to get rid of these prison uniforms,' Rhidian said, staring at the material with distaste.

'I agree,' Rebus said. 'It's been far too long for me wearing these horrible orange boiler suits. They must have had someone who was really depressed to pick the worst colour they could think of.'

'The crew have fresh clothes on board. I'm sure we can all find something to fit us,' Caleb added. 'I've been in these clothes for a while, too. They have a shower room on board too, but I never had a chance to use it, obviously not wanting to get caught,' Caleb said honestly.

'Look, there's no fear of them catching up with us anytime soon. So we can relax, just for a bit. After we've eaten, we can go and look for something more comfortable to wear,' Rhidian said as he swallowed a mouthful of orange juice. 'What do you say Red?'

Red had been quiet while the others talked and it felt good being included in the conversation. He had taken a liking to Rhidian from the start because he treated him mostly like an adult. Rebus, on the other hand, was older and had that old-school way about him, which annoyed the hell out of Red. And he hated being called a boy, which Rebus used towards him regularly. Red was also getting a bad vibe from the newly found Caleb, who took every opportunity to take the mickey.

'Yeah, wearing something different to this old thing would be great.' The suit Red was wearing was really baggy and not meant for a boy to wear. In fact, he looked more ridiculous than the others.

'Let's get cleaned up and changed. I'm sure we could all do with a nice shower,' Rhidian assumed. 'We'd have to take turns though to steer the ship. It's quite easy really.' Caleb and Red looked on reluctantly. 'We obviously have to keep an eye out just in case someone does spot us,' Rhidian said.

'That would make sense,' Rebus added with encouragement. 'We don't want anyone sneaking up on us,' he said, as he partially eyed Caleb and smiled. Caleb peered back and gave a grin.

They all mostly found something that fitted them, and when it was Rhidian's turn to shower and change, Rebus steered the ship for a while.

Luckily, for the boy, there was a crewmember with his size and he found a pair of jeans and a T-shirt that kind of suited him. He also managed to find a pair of black trainers. The others also found something to wear and they all met up in the control room, where Rhidian had taken back over from Rebus.

'Why don't you all get some sleep, and I'll keep a look out,' Rhidian said.

'How are we going to do this, Rhidian? You're going to have to rest at some point,' Rebus said. 'You'll have to show the rest of us how to pilot this ship properly in order for you to get some sleep too,' Rebus added.

'Wake me in a couple of hours, Rhidian, and I can take over from you. I'm not sure if I'm any good,' Caleb added, 'but you can show us all the proper way to guide this ship tomorrow.'

'Oh right, that's great, we can share the job.' Rhidian was delighted; he had thoughts of navigating for hours on end with no relief.

'Err, wake me instead, will you? I can pilot the ship.' Rebus looked at Rhidian with a penetrating glare.

'What's the matter, old man? Don't you trust me?' Caleb questioned with suspicion, and gave Rebus a look of distaste.

'Look, Caleb, we can't be too careful. We don't know you from Adam,' Rebus added honestly. 'We were all locked up in Skytraz and you weren't. It'll take us a bit of time to get used to having you on board.'

'I understand. That's fair enough. I could be a spy and turn this ship around, taking us all back to the authorities,' Caleb said. 'But, Rebus, I'm not. I honestly do not want to get caught either. I'm in the same boat as you three. I'm running away from something too, and I don't want to go back.'

'Understood,' Rebus agreed, 'but what are you running from?'

'Rebus,' Rhidian interrupted, 'that's not our business really, is it? We should respect one another or this trip is going to be a long one. With no respect for each other things will get very awkward, very quickly.'

'I know,' Rebus said, 'but I'd still like to do this shift on my own.'

'Well, look, after tonight we can share the shifts in pairs. We will all have to trust one another at some point, don't you agree, Rebus?' Rhidian urged, and Rebus nodded reluctantly. 'You and Caleb can do one and Red and I can do the other. Is everyone happy with that?' There were general nods from each of them.

'I suppose so,' Rebus agreed reluctantly.

'We do have another problem though,' Rhidian added.

'What's that?' Red asked with curiosity.

'Where exactly are we headed?' Rhidian said, as he looked at Rebus. 'We've broken away from Skytraz Prison, but we're just drifting into nowhere really.'

'Just keep us on this path and I'm sure by tomorrow I'll know where to head,' Rebus assured them. Rhidian shrugged his shoulders and nodded; he realised that he had to trust the wizard.

'Go and get some sleep you lot,' Rhidian urged, and everyone went off to separate cabins, leaving the engineer alone in the control room to ponder.

Chapter 11
Ghost Ship

Evening casually wafted in and with it a dense mist that engulfed everything in its path. The air was warm but the fog carried a fresh and instant dampness that coated the ship in a glistening, silver skin. It was virtually impossible for Rhidian to see where he was going. The swirling grey shapes danced and caressed the ship's hull and spattered the windows with its spray.

'Where did *this* come from?' Rhidian whispered to himself. The others were sleeping in their quarters. 'I can't see a damn thing,' he grunted. 'I've got to stop before I crash into something.' He reluctantly switched off the engine and let the vessel drift along at its own pace – the propeller at the rear slowed to a stop.

The engineer lent forward and wiped the window using his sleeve as a cloth. He half closed his eyes and tried to see beyond the ship's bough. The lights that peppered the vessel's outline were just a decoration and didn't seem to penetrate the weather.

'This is useless,' he groaned and rubbed harder as if it made any difference. Rhidian could just about feel the last motion of the ship before it settled. All that could be heard now was the creaking timbers and hiss of a breeze.

Suddenly there was a dull thud! The whole ship shuddered and was followed by the sound of grinding wood. Rhidian was slightly shaken by the impact and looked out of the window again but still couldn't make out anything. He had to investigate, but there couldn't be any damage because they were barely moving, he assumed.

He opened the cabin door and steadily walked onto the deck. The wisps of cold mist wet his face and he angrily wiped them away from his mouth in disgust, as if it were cobwebs. The darkness combined with the grey made it difficult to see. He stood silently and wondered if the impact had woken the others. He was also intrigued as to what he might find – it scared him.

The fog began to thin and Rhidian felt that something strange was about to happen. The mist swirled before his eyes and revealed a large darkened shape. He realised right away that it was another ship.

'Oh crap,' he rasped. He didn't know what to do. Should he wake up the others, if they weren't awake already? But none of his crew came running onto the deck.

His thoughts went back to the matter at hand. Where were the crew? If this ship had been following them since the break out, why wasn't he already arrested and his friends rounded up? No, there must be some other explanation. Rhidian noticed that the vessel had kind of wedged itself against their ship.

He approached the handrail and peered onto the deck of the other craft. It was really difficult to see anything specific. The blackness engulfed everything like a blanket. It was quiet too, an eerie and unnerving silence except for creaking timbers, which he was getting used to. Rhidian was more curious than scared at this point. It appeared, though, that there was no one on board – a ghost ship!

What should he do? Should he leave it and start his own engine back up and pull away? There was a deep urge for him to board the empty vessel and investigate. What harm could it do? He couldn't really travel anywhere tonight in this thick fog anyway.

'H-Hello,' he called out tentatively, hot air rising from his open mouth. But his thin voice was swallowed in an instant by the denseness of the air. He could feel his heart race in his chest. Rhidian decided that a quick investigation wouldn't hurt. He breathed in deeply and a smile masked his nervousness. He climbed over the threshold and planted his feet on the inviting deck.

'H-Hello.' He stopped and cleared his throat. 'Hello, is there anyone there?' he called out with more purpose to his voice, but nothing came back. There can't be anyone on board, surely, or they would have responded by now, he reasoned, and decided there was nothing else to do but to explore further.

He was totally damp from the swirling mist and the cold feel of his clothes made him shiver. A watery moon grinned through a fading patch of clouds, slightly illuminating the deck. Then... what was that?

*****

Red flicked open his tired eyes, not quite sure what he'd been dreaming about. He sat up and his head hit the upper bunk with a numbing jolt.

'Aw, great,' he groaned, and rubbed the sore spot vigorously. He felt thirsty and tried to swallow, but his throat was too dry. He suddenly thought of the fridge in the kitchen and relished the idea of a cool drink and maybe a snack too. The youngster forgot about his sore head and climbed out of his bunk. The good thing about this ship was the fact that everyone had a room each. He opened the cabin door as quietly as possible, but it still let out a high-pitched squeak, no matter how gently he pulled at it. He creased up his face and squinted his eyes, as if that would stop the noise happening. When the gap was wide enough, he slipped through.

Strangely, when he closed the door behind him, it didn't make any noise. He shook his head in disbelief. Once outside, he tiptoed along the dark corridor and out through another door onto the deck. Every time he was out here it made him feel calm for some strange reason; he couldn't explain why. The moon was beaming down and the mist had thinned. There was a breeze and he drank it in as if it were a glass of water. He then realised that the sky ship wasn't moving! Why hadn't he noticed this before? The calm throb of the engine was a comforting sound, but now there was just dead air. He stood pondering – something was wrong, he could feel it.

Then, came the realisation! How hadn't he noticed it sooner? He looked up and the sight made his jaw fall open.

'Good grief,' he gasped. There was a ship, right there. The first thing he felt was panic. He was trembling, but wasn't sure if it was the sudden cold or his nerves. Then he thought… Rhidian!

'Rhidian, yes, Rhidian would know what to do,' he mumbled. The boy quickly made his way to the control room. But Rhidian wasn't there.

Where was he? He stepped back onto the deck and scuttled around in a bid to find him.

'Rhidian? Rhidian?' he called out as quietly as he could. Where is he? That was when he thought he saw something move on the *other* ship. He stopped panicking and stared out onto the other deck. The moon had just disappeared behind a bank of clouds and so everything was left in twilight. But there was definitely something moving over there.

'Rhidian, is that you?' His voice was louder than he'd intended. The figure didn't respond. Red, filled with curiosity and fear, wandered over towards the port side of his ship. Maybe he's in trouble, he thought. 'I'm coming over,' Red said with conviction.

*****

Rebus roused from slumber; he'd been in a deep sleep but, whatever woke him, it wasn't good. He, being a wizard, felt certain forces and this definitely felt evil. It had been such a long time since he'd last felt something spiritual. His magical powers had lay dormant and now were tingling. But strangely he felt two sources of power – one good and one evil. He quickly got to his feet and made his way outside. He was also sensing someone else was already out there and saw that it was Caleb.

'What's going on?' Rebus asked, his voice filled with suspicion.

'I don't really know, except for that,' Caleb said, and pointed directly to the ship that had drifted into them. 'I can't find Red or Rhidian,' he continued. 'What are you thinking?'

'I'm thinking that you are a wizard and what woke me woke you too,' Rebus said simply. Caleb stood for a moment and said nothing.

'OK,' he finally relented, 'I am.'

'I knew it,' Rebus hissed, as if he'd won some bet. 'I had that feeling when we first met, but I haven't used my powers for so long that I wasn't sure.'

'Well, now you know. So?' Caleb said, expecting a reply.

'So, you and I know what is on that ship,' Rebus said, peering straight into Caleb's eyes. He peered back unblinking.

'Ghosts, spirits – trapped for eternity?'

'Yep, I believe so and they've probably got Rhidian and Red held prisoner,' Rebus assumed.

'I think you're right,' Caleb agreed.

'How are we going to do this? You got a plan?' Rebus asked.

'Well, they don't actually know we're wizards, do they? That at least gives us the upper hand,' Caleb said.

'We need to do something first though,' Rebus added.

'Yes, we have to protect ourselves,' Caleb acknowledged.

'Not here though,' Rebus continued.

'No, it has to be away from sight,' Caleb agreed. The two figures moved around the control room, away from the ghost ship. They stood on the starboard side, out of the moon's rays. The two sorcerers reached out and touched each other's hands. There was a yellow glow that passed between them. It only lasted a matter of seconds before it dissipated, but that was all they needed.

'Now we're ready,' Rebus said with confidence.

'Let's go then.' Caleb wasn't one to wait around.

The wizards made their way to port side and climbed over onto the other vessel. Once there, they were immediately confronted by a series of glowing figures.

'A welcome committee,' Rebus said. A grin formed on his face.

'Yep, looks like.' Caleb held the same look.

'How do we communicate with these, uh, beings? I'm a little rusty,' Rebus admitted, feeling awkward. One of the luminous figures glided forward. Caleb looked at it. It was the shape of a man but with a blurred glow around the edges. The skull face was a milky-white and the soft shimmer around its body soon disappeared into the murky black robe of its torso.

'Yep, ghosts,' Caleb announced.

'Come on... really? How did you work that one out?' Rebus mused.

'You are our prisoners now,' came the thin rasping voice of the skeletal captain.

'Um, err, I don't think so,' Caleb responded sharply. 'You may have our friends, but you won't take us any time soon.'

Suddenly more of them came from the shadows and immediately circled the wizards. Once all eight of them were in place, they linked hands and forged a solid connection – a white circle. Rebus rolled his eyes in Caleb's direction with a look of concern. Soon, a white light emerged from the pirate crew that bleached everything around the two ships.

'We need to work against this now, Rebus,' Caleb said, but he wasn't looking so smug now.

'Agreed,' Rebus said. 'Deflecting spell?' the old wizard added quickly. There was a quick nod of reaction from his colleague. They worked together for the first time as a team by pressing their index fingers to their temples. Rebus could instantly feel his fellow wizard swim through his mind. And, Caleb had exactly the same experience with Rebus. The connection of mind transference emitted a magical, invisible beam. This counteracted the ghosts' attempt to overpower them. The two opposite energies pushed against one another in a light display of sharp, exploding sparks and a thunderous boom.

'We've got to keep a hold of this!' Caleb yelled, the brilliance of the enemy surge bleaching his face to a ghostly skull.

'Keep your mind free of anything else and let yourself immerse in the moment.' Rebus' tranquil voice calmly washed through the younger wizard's thoughts. The ghostly crew intensified their force but it was no match for the wizard's magic and, eventually, their strength of mind overwhelmed and destroyed their ghostly powers. The once-blinding supernatural magic of the ghost crew diminished into a milky glow and finally absorbed back into them. Rebus' and Caleb's spell had worked. The captain's eyeless sockets peered back as the being stood defiant. Caleb returned the glare, unflinching, but inside he and Rebus were weakened by the tussle.

'Who are you?' the stunned captain bleated. His crew parted, broke away and floated in line behind their leader. 'You are not true men.'

'No, we are wizards,' Caleb said with pride, 'and your deathly powers are no match for ours.' Caleb felt Rebus in his head again. 'We can't sustain another attack. We need time to build our magic.' Caleb knew this too.

'Give back our friends,' Rebus ordered.

'We will not give up our prisoners, but you are free to go,' the ghost captain insisted.

'That's never going to happen,' Caleb shot back. 'Do you want us to show you exactly what we can do?' He raised his shoulders and puffed out his chest. Rebus looked on with suspicion.

'What are you doing?' Rebus mumbled out of the corner of his mouth.

'Shut up and follow my lead,' Caleb said, still looking straight into the gaunt, bony face of his enemy. Caleb started waving his arms and howling like a demented wolf.

'The powers that be will diminish thee,' Caleb ranted. Rebus followed his lead. The ghosts themselves looked disorientated; they knew that the power they held didn't work.

'Stop... do not continue,' the zombie captain screeched in surrender. 'We will return your shipmates.' The two sorcerers ceased their ridiculous charade and knew it had worked. They momentarily glanced at each other with a look of relief.

The captain must have given a couple of his men a signal, because some of them broke away from the others and disappeared below deck. Rebus and Caleb stood in silence and out of breath. Sure enough, the captain's men returned with the two prisoners – Rhidian and Red. They slowly walked behind the ghosts – the both of them were in a kind of trance. They were engulfed in a swirling, smoky veil. Rebus looked at them, then half squinted with a look of distaste at the ghost captain.

'Release them,' he ordered. The dead crewmembers somehow urged the humans forward to the centre of the deck. They circled them in a clockwise motion – Red and Rhidian didn't even blink. The ghosts swirled and picked up speed as they danced around their victims in a grey blur. Eventually, there was nothing more than wisps of mist. The hypnotic hold that trapped Red and Rhidian lifted. It was as if they'd been frozen and instantly defrosted. The engineer and the boy fell to their knees, the weakness in their limbs obvious. The wizards moved in to help them.

'Rebus… Caleb… What happened?' Rhidian mumbled, trying to find the strength to speak a full sentence. Red couldn't even do that – he was drained. Caleb looked up and saw that the ghosts were slowly evaporating into the woodwork.

'Rebus, we have to get them out of here now,' Caleb said with urgency. They helped them quickly to their feet and dragged them to the side of the ship. Without looking back they flung them onto the deck of their own ship. Rebus and Caleb quickly followed, and as soon as they cleared the ghost ship, it began to fade. Rhidian and Red lay on the deck, still in a stupor. The wizards stood side-by-side, witnessing the final remains of the ghost ship vanish. Then there was almost nothing, only the groans of the released prisoners.

'Rebus, what happened?' Rhidian asked when he could eventually find his voice.

'We were nearly all captured, that's what happened. From now on, if you see anything suspicious, inform me straight away,' Rebus said bluntly.

'Yeah… yeah, we will,' Rhidian said.

'Right, I have to tell you something,' Rebus announced. By now, Rhidian and Red were on their feet, but still unstable.

'What's up Rebus? Besides another near-death experience?' Rhidian said flippantly.

'This is just to inform you that Caleb… well, he's the same as me.'

'What, old?' Red joked, but when he saw the look from Rebus, bowed his head sheepishly. Caleb bit his lip in a bid not to laugh.

'He's a wizard.' Rebus rolled his eyes from one to the other, waiting for either Red or Rhidian to give a smart quip. 'If it hadn't been for Caleb, then we would all have been captured,' he added. 'The power from that ghost ship was too much for me to handle alone. My powers are still building.'

'Well, err, that's good that we have two wizards on board,' Rhidian realised. 'Twice the experience and power.' Rhidian looked at the boy. 'I thank you both for your help.' Rhidian prodded the boy.

'Yeah, me too,' Red said with a vigorous nod. Rebus turned to Caleb.

'Do you want to continue with us? I mean, you have the power to do and go as you please really.' Rebus waited for a response from his new colleague.

'I'm willing to help you find whatever you're looking for,' Caleb spoke up. 'I'll have to see what my future holds after that.'

'Caleb, can you teach me,' Red chipped in, 'to do magic?'

'You can't teach someone magic, young lad,' Rebus interrupted. 'It has to be something already inside you.' Red rolled his eyes. Rebus, it seemed, was always putting him down.

'We'll see, Red,' Caleb said, realising the tension between them. 'Maybe I can teach you a little.' Red's eyes lit up and a real smile filled his face.

'We have to get out of here, now. Time is of the essence,' Rebus said, as he made his way to the control room. 'Come on, you lot, we've a mission to fulfil. No dawdling, get a move on.' The rest of them rolled their eyes and nodded in compliance.

'Come on,' Rhidian urged as they followed the old wizard.

'That was close,' Red whispered to the engineer. 'I don't want to go through that again.'

'Too close, lad. We're lucky. It could have turned out a lot worse,' Rhidian said. Rebus shouted to them from the control room. 'Come on, we don't want another telling off, do we?' He grinned. Once they were all inside, Rhidian started the engine and the big craft pulled away.

'I'll take over now,' Rebus insisted.

'Look, why don't you two get a full sleep?' Rhidian insisted, pointing to Rebus and Caleb. 'I'll continue steering through this fog and I'll keep Red with me for company. I feel totally awake now anyway. In the morning, you and Caleb can take over while we sleep. It'll be easier to pilot the ship when you can see clearly ahead, don't you think?' Rhidian looked at the two wizards and they agreed with a nod. So Rhidian gripped the wheel as Red sat in one of the chairs, whilst the others went back to their rooms.

Chapter 12
The Vision

The early light of morning cracked through the thinning cloud line. The awakening sun lazily cast a pale yellow rectangle on the cabin floor. The heat was already rising and by midday it would be scorching. Rhidian was leaning against a side panel, half asleep; all the fear and excitement had taken its toll. Red was dozing in the corner.

Caleb walked in and stood by the side of the skipper.

'Morning, Rhidian,' he said. Rhidian flinched. He hadn't realised Caleb was standing there.

'Oh, good morning, Caleb,' Rhidian replied, eyes still at half-mast. 'So, you're a wizard, too?' He tried to make conversation and stay awake at the same time, but still stifled a yawn.

'Yes, Rhidian, sorry to have been so secretive,' Caleb replied. 'I couldn't reveal who I really was until I knew exactly who I was dealing with. I was lucky to get away from Jenta-Lor.' As he said the name, a jolt of nerves shot through Rhidian's stomach. 'I would have probably ended up in the same position as you and the others if I'd been caught,' the wizard continued.

'I totally understand. Jenta-Lor imprisoned me under false pretences. He's imprisoned a lot of innocent people and wizards.' As Rhidian said the words, he went quiet for a moment. He looked straight ahead but didn't really see anything, only the blue, hazy sky. All he could conjure was an image of his beautiful wife, Mia – her eyes glazed, and lips pursed. He felt a lump in his throat and swallowed it down. He was tired and at his most vulnerable. He snuffled up the streams that began to form in his nostrils and wiped his nose on the back of his sleeve. He came back out of his thoughts. 'Oh, thanks again by the way.'

'For what?' Caleb asked, arching his brow.

'For helping to rescue us,' Rhidian continued. 'I'd hate to think what life Red and I would have had on that ship.' He wiped the excess tears from his eyes, hiding his face from the wizard.

'You wouldn't have stayed alive much longer, I'm afraid,' Caleb admitted bluntly.

'Why? What would they have done to us?' Rhidian pressed, uncertain as to what the answer was going to be.

'You were both due to be… let's just say you would have joined the crew, whether you wanted to or not,' Caleb said, sounding really ominous. Rhidian looked serious for a moment.

'You mean they would have taken our souls and made us into... one of them?' He gasped and opened his mouth in shock.

'I'm afraid so,' Caleb added. Rhidian stroked his chin and suddenly he didn't feel quite as tired as he had been, pondering on what might have been.

'Those pirates are the least of our problems,' Rebus spoke as he entered the room; the tempo of the conversation took an even more sinister path. 'Believe me, there will be darker times ahead.'

'So what now?' Red said dryly as he flicked open his eyes.

'For you two, a few hours' sleep,' Rebus insisted.

'Yes, you should both get some rest,' Caleb said as he took the helm.

'You won't get an argument from me,' Rhidian said, yawning again.

'We'll take it from here,' Rebus added. 'Go on, off you go.'

'Okay. Just keep her straight and if you come across anything unusual, or there's a problem with the engines, wake me up.'

'We've got it from here,' Rebus said, gently nodding his head.

'All right, see you later. Come on, Red.' Rhidian said to the boy and they waved as they made their way to the cabins. Caleb steered as best as he could and Rebus stood at his side. Rebus loved the grunt and vibration from the ship's heart. It was way different to the stone-cold feel of the prison: damp walls and lifeless inmates.

'OK, push that handle.' Rebus indicated a lever on the console. Caleb pushed the throttle forward, the engine growled into life and the sudden motion made Rebus grab for something solid to keep his balance. 'Easy. Be a bit more gentle. She's very sensitive,' he said.

'S-sorry, it's the first time I've ever done this,' he admitted sheepishly.

'It's OK, just ease it back a little.' Caleb did as he was asked and the revs dropped. 'Keep it like that for a while,' Rebus instructed.

'You've done this before?' Caleb said with interest.

'Not for a long time, but it's coming back to me.' He smiled and Caleb grinned back. 'You were on Valusha then?' Rebus probed, raising his voice to combat the revs of the motor.

'Yes-yes I was,' Caleb repeated, and lifted his voice, wondering what was coming next. Rebus paused and slowly rolled his eyes, trying to catch Caleb's full attention.

'How come I never saw you there?' Rebus quizzed with a hint of suspicion.

'Am I under investigation now?' Caleb snapped back and creased his face. He thought he'd already proved himself.

'No-no, just general conversation.' Rebus widened his mouth to a smile. 'Nothing more.'

'Okay.' Caleb took time to collect his thoughts before explaining himself.

'Well,' Rebus badgered, waiting for an answer.

'All right, all right,' Caleb finally relented. 'I entered Valusha at the peak of all the troubles.' Rebus listened intently. 'I felt the force that dampened my powers straight away as I entered the city. So, I masked them so that I wouldn't be found out. As you know, the whole place was in disarray, so I hid as soon as I could. I mixed in with the population and no one suspected who I was.'

The wizard kept his eyes dead ahead when he spoke. 'Over the next few days, I noticed people escaping and realised that they were wizards too. As you know...' Caleb turned his head slightly and looked at Rebus, 'even if a wizard's powers are useless in a certain situation then another wizard can still tell that they are a sorcerer.' Rebus nodded in agreement.

'I continued to blend in with the locals and found work doing odd jobs. I stayed there for a year or so, but I could see things were getting worse with the new overlord and knew I had to leave. I got to know the different crew members that came to port. I gave one a couple of bottles of wine one night and waited for him to go to sleep whilst he was on watch duty. So, I stowed away on the ship. My plan was to slip off the ship unseen and start somewhere else.'

Caleb turned to Rebus and looked deeply into his eyes. 'That's the truth,' he said, and didn't flinch when he said it. Caleb could see Rebus weighing things up in his mind. And then, he blinked.

'Ok… I believe you,' Rebus said, finally giving in.

'So, where are we headed?' Caleb asked.

'I've an important mission, Caleb.' Rebus now spoke with a real importance to his tone. 'I have to find someone called Obsidian.' When the name left Rebus' lips there was a flash of recognition in Caleb's demeanour – his eyes narrowed and his breathing quickened. 'You know Obsidian?' Rebus questioned.

'I don't know him, but I'd heard all about Obsidian when I was working in Valusha. Everyone seemed sad to lose him – even though it was the population who voted in Jenta-Lor in the first place,' Caleb said.

'I'm sure he hypnotised them somehow. Obsidian was a good leader,' Rebus added with a glare. 'I have to find him and the rest of the wizards, whoever is left, and take back Valusha.' Rebus looked grave. 'What are your plans now?'

'I only want a quiet life. This Jenta-Lor is an evil influence on everybody. There totally isn't any need for that brutish police force,' Caleb said with conviction. 'If you want to get Valusha back for wizards to rule it once more... then I'm with you. Maybe I could make a life there if peace is restored.'

Caleb turned fully to Rebus and a smile engulfed both wizards.

'Finding Obsidian isn't going to be easy,' Rebus said with a shake of his head. 'Give me your hand?' Caleb held out his hand and Rebus grasped it. They stood on deck, eyes closed. The connection between the two sorcerers was strong. An apparition slowly formed in their minds. There appeared a bright mist, and a figure pushed through the white curtain. It soon stood out against the background in solid form. Rebus felt a tightening of his stomach, a joyous feeling.

It was Obsidian. Even though Rebus' eyes were shut, he felt himself smile. He wanted to speak to him, but it was only a connection of minds. Obsidian looked unhappy and alone. This tugged at Rebus' heart. Obsidian and Rebus were great friends in Valusha and Caleb could feel the connection with both of them. The experience didn't last and the image soon disappeared. Rebus felt himself sigh and he blinked his eyes open again. The smile was replaced by a frown. Caleb opened his eyes too and saw the sadness.

'Did you…?' Rebus was about to ask.

'Yes,' Caleb replied, not giving him the chance. 'North, we have to head north.'

'Yes… north.' Rebus nodded as he still tried to keep the image of Obsidian in his mind. But it was like trying to capture smoke. He grimaced. He'd spent far too long in that prison – it had dulled his senses. He had to get Valusha back and Obsidian was the only real leader who could do this task.

Did *he* want to though, that was another question. Now it was the time of wizards once again. 'Definitely north, to the Outlands,' Rebus said with purpose; he'd never felt so determined in his entire life.

Chapter 13
Cloud Hopper

Red was already on the deck when Rhidian finally left his cabin. The warm evening breeze was welcomed after being cooped up in the small room. Rhidian glanced across the expanse and all he could see was the powder-blue sky. The ship was moving at a steady rate of knots (he could feel the chug-chug-chug of the engine through the flooring), and for the first time he felt relaxed. He saw Red standing there, on the deck, perfectly still. Something was up. He could tell by the way he was grinning. Rhidian peered at him through half-open eyes.

'What are you smiling about?' he felt compelled to ask. Red burst out laughing when Rhidian questioned him. 'What?' Rhidian was completely mystified.

'Okay,' he giggled, 'what's the name of this ship?' He leaned against the side and waited for the answer. Rhidian frowned because he was taken completely by surprise.

'Uh, err, I have to say... I don't know,' he answered honestly.

'Yes... I knew it,' Red responded, almost dancing on the wooden floor, punching the air. 'We've all been on this ship for days and I'll bet no one knows what it's called.' Rhidian looked at the boy, and it was nice to see him being playful; after all, he was really just a kid. He thought back to the first time he'd seen him in the prison. Red was terrified back then. He was a boy in a man's world. This sent a shiver through Rhidian's whole body.

'All right, smarty-pants... what *is* it called?' Rhidian waited for the answer; he realised that Red already knew. The boy held back for a moment, for effect, and Rhidian peered back at him – then the waiting got too much.

'Red... well, what's it called? I haven't got all day you know,' Rhidian said impatiently.

'*Cloud Hopper*,' Red announced with an air of importance and looked really pleased with himself.

'Oh, okay, great name,' Rhidian said, and didn't get the joke. He still didn't know why it was so funny as he walked into the control room. He saw Caleb and Rebus studying a chart with great interest.

'Hi boys, where we headed? Did you have any problems?' Rhidian asked and broke their concentration. They looked up and gave him a welcome nod. He returned the gesture, rubbing his chin.

'Sleep well?' Caleb asked.

'Yes, thanks, I really did.'

'No, we haven't hit any problems. Rebus was on top of it. Apparently, he worked on these things years ago,' Caleb reported.

'Oh, great,' Rhidian said, happy in the knowledge that he could get the same rest as everyone else.

'We're going to head to the north – Gelbar, in fact,' Rebus revealed. 'It seems the best option.'

'Gelbar.' Rhidian scratched his cheek. 'Don't think I've ever heard of it, but all right. Why there? Have you sensed something?'

'We think that Obsidian may be there, hopefully,' Caleb chipped in.

'You want to take over and keep her steady on this course?' Rebus was pointing at a map.

'I'm not really a sailor. All I know is how to maintain and repair things,' Rhidian admitted. 'I can steer, but you'll have to bear with me on the navigation side of things.'

'No problem.' Rebus seemed confident. 'Keep her on these co-ordinates,' he said, as he moved his finger to the navigation setting that he'd already put in.

Rhidian studied the map intently. 'It's simple really, just keep the ship in line with this.' Caleb showed him by indicating the clock-face dial with a needle inside. The needle was leading the way. 'Stay to this and the ship will stay true.'

'So, all I have to do is follow your settings and make sure I don't deviate? Seems simple enough, just like you said.' Rhidian nodded his approval and added, 'Do you know what this ship is called?'

'*Cloud Hopper,*' Caleb replied smartly, and Rhidian's expectations sank. 'Why?'

'Oh, no reason,' he said, feeling rather sheepish. Red grinned at Caleb as he stood at the back of the cabin.

'Red,' Rebus called out, 'can you sort some food for us all?'

'Yes, right away.' Rhidian heard the quick reaction from the teenager and chuckled. That boy is always hungry, he thought.

Caleb stepped away from the wheel and strolled outside and onto the deck. Rhidian noticed him making his way towards the bow. The sorcerer stood at dead centre, just looking out into the wide-open spaces. Rhidian kept on looking at his back; the wizard didn't move. Soon he was joined by Rebus, and Rhidian looked on curiously. They were standing side by side like two commanders surveying a battle – something was up, Rhidian could feel it. They turned at the same time, both wearing grave faces. They entered the control room, Rebus first and then Caleb following.

'What's happening?' A concerned Rhidian posed the question.

'We have some problems,' Rebus spoke first.

'What kind of problems? Come on, spit it out. We're all in this together,' Rhidian said, feeling agitated.

'There's a storm ahead, for one,' Caleb added. 'A violent storm, we're sure of it.' He was rubbing his chin and looked worried.

'What's the other?' Rhidian asked, thinking a violent storm was bad enough.

'We are being followed,' Rebus said, his bearded, grim face hard to read.

'Followed? By who? Jenta-Lor?' Rhidian was getting more anxious by the second.

'We're not really sure, but they're gaining on us,' Caleb said.

'How long have you known this? What can we do?' Rhidian was an engineer not a strategist in military manoeuvres.

'We haven't known for long. We kind of felt it at first… it's a wizard thing. Well, we can't outrun them in a cargo ship, that's for sure,' Rebus said simply. 'We're going to have to ride the storm and hope we lose them. Oh, and not get smashed up in the process,' he added.

'We'll have to give it full engine revs – give it all we've got,' Rhidian pressed.

'We can't. We don't want to blow the engine,' Caleb added.

'I'll repair it later if it does break down, but we've no choice now. If they catch us… it won't matter anyway,' Rhidian said gravely. At that point Red walked in with a tray of food and a grim look on his face too.

'What's up, Red?' Rhidian said.

'Th-there's someone following us I think,' he stammered. Rhidian, Caleb and Rebus burst out onto the deck. The wizards were right – they were being followed.

Far in the distance was a dark speck against the blue backdrop which was gradually getting bigger and bigger by the second.

'They're gaining at a rate of knots,' Rebus realised. 'We have to try and outmanoeuvre them.'

'Oh, good grief, what kind of ship is that?' Rhidian gasped. 'We've only just escaped a bloody ghost ship,' he cursed. He ran back into the control room and emerged with a pair of binoculars.

Rhidian lifted the lens to his eyes and adjusted the focus. Now he could see it plainly. It was an older vessel with a large balloon on top keeping it afloat. At least it has a weakness, Rhidian thought. The flag revealed a white background with a pair of crossed swords. 'I don't recognise the insignia.'

'Let me look.' Caleb gestured to Rhidian and tugged at his shirt. Rhidian handed it over and

Caleb studied hard. 'I would hazard to guess that it's a pirate ship. I've seen that insignia before.'

'Great,' Rebus moaned. 'Okay, no time to mess around. We have to get out of here.'

The cool summer breeze that had gently caressed their ship soon began to whip up into a chopping wind, making the vessel list.

'What's happening now?' Red shouted.

'That.' Rebus pointed towards the bow and the storm that was fast erupting ahead of them. In the distance were fierce black clouds and huge spears of lightning. There was a sudden and deafening crack of thunder to add to the confusion.

'Oh, good grief,' Red exclaimed, almost transfixed to the spot. 'How did that happen so quickly?'

'I'll take the helm!' Rebus screeched as he dashed to the control room. 'Find something to hold onto when you get inside. It's going to be a rough ride.'

'I'll give you a hand. You're going to need all the help you can get to steady this thing,' Rhidian said, his voice sounding hoarse.

They all dived into the control room. Rebus and Rhidian were at the wheel. Red and Caleb standing each side of them.

'We need more speed,' Rebus growled and pushed the lever to maximum. The engine lifted its revs with a huge roar, and the *Cloud Hopper* surged forward, the whole ship vibrating under such power.

Red peered through the back window and saw the pirate ship looming in the background. He felt his nerves twist in his stomach. He swallowed hard and turned to the others. Even though the cargo ship was at full speed, it was no match for the pirate vessel.

'It's gaining on us!' Red screamed, but with the storm in full flow and the ship buffeting in the winds, it was hard to hear him.

'Hold on, everyone, we're going into the storm any second now,' Rebus said, and appeared calm. He knew there was nothing more they could do. The bright, blue sky had already morphed into a murky, black hell. Bright, blinding flashes ripped through the cabin like a rapier, followed by the deafening boom of a wild thunder. Strong, gusting winds came out of nowhere and slammed against the vessel. Objects slid from side-to-side as the tray of food that Red had prepared crashed to the floor and threw its contents in all directions. Rain burst from inside the darkness and bombarded the cargo vessel with a torrential downpour.

Rhidian and Rebus wrestled the wheel as it tried to pull away from their grip. The ship rattled and rolled inside the vast, black monsoon. Sharp jabs of violent wind threw uppercuts to its mid-rift, as if in a boxing match. Red fell to the floor and slid towards the open door, his mouth wide in a scream but nothing came out.

Caleb saw what was happening and reached out to grab his leg. He managed to grip at his ankle and the wizard scrambled to a handrail to hold on to. The boy eventually found his voice and called out, but no one could hear him in the din.

Rhidian strained as he and Rebus held onto the wheel – like two gladiators who were arm wrestling a bear – the tension on their faces clear. Rhidian pulled as Rebus pushed – both tried to right the ship.

'Don't let go, don't let go!' Rebus repeatedly screamed as he tried to keep hold his end. Rhidian peered back at Rebus and saw his face light up from a blinding lightning strike. He looked ghostly, which scared the life out of the engineer, but he held on regardless.

Caleb had meanwhile jammed his heel against the doorpost and wedged himself in a position to help Red. He pulled with all his might to get the boy back inside the room. Red tried to push his body back, but when he saw a loose barrel tumble along the deck towards him, he stared in wild horror, not able to do anything about it.

'HELP ME SOMEONE!' he screeched and threw his arms in front of his face for protection. Caleb gave one enormous yank and pulled the boy back inside as the barrel rolled past and broke through the ship's side panel and disappeared into the storm. Red twisted onto his back and grabbed the same steel rail that Caleb was clamped to. He let out a heavy-winded sigh, not even able to acknowledge Caleb for what he'd just done. Red's hair was plastered to his head and the top half of his shirt was dark from the soaking, but he was alive. He sobbed and his heart pounded in his chest. He closed his eyes as tight as he could and held on for dear life.

'HOLD ON EVERYONE... HERE WE GO!' Rhidian shouted – his arm muscles burned from the heavy grip. The *Cloud Hopper* was soon swallowed up and lost in the depth of the squall.

Chapter 14
Crash Landing

This was it. Rebus and Rhidian held onto the wheel with all their might and tried to keep the *Cloud Hopper* steady. Caleb and Red held on as best they could. The sky ship tossed and jarred as if on a stormy sea – except this was in the sky and the only way out was a deathly fall. In all the confusion, everyone had forgotten about the ship that was pursuing them.

The enemy vessel was only a matter of a quarter mile behind and gaining, but it also struggled against the terrible weather conditions. The lights suddenly went out on the *Cloud Hopper*, leaving the control room in blackness. There was a resounding screech from Red when something hit him. The sounds of loose debris rang out as things crashed against cupboards and crockery smashed all around.

'Are you okay?' Celeb shouted from the gloom.

'Yes-yes I'm fine,' came the ominous reply from the youngster. A huge flash of fork lightning erupted over the ship and bleached the faces of each crewmember in bright white. The blinding flash was followed by the loudest eruption of thunder that shook the ship to its very core.

'Jeez, that was close!' Red screamed; his nerves had got the better of him.

'Hold on, boy, there'll be a lot more to come,' Rebus shouted and Red rolled his eyes with contempt. 'Don't give me that look, boy,' Rebus growled. Red was shocked. How on earth did he see me? he thought. 'I can see everything,' Rebus lied, and just assumed the boy was doing his usual face pulling. Red stopped making faces and concentrated on holding on.

The wind was using the *Cloud Hopper* as a toy, flipping and tossing it from side to side.

'Can't you and Caleb do something magically?' Rhidian shouted into Rebus' ear. 'You've got the power, surely?'

'No, Mother Nature is a strong force to deal with,' the wizard answered. 'It's too powerful, even for the likes of us wizards,' he said. With that, another electrical surge burst across the sky and lit up the entire region. Rebus managed to look across the room through the window. He was shocked to see the pirate ship within range to board them.

'We've got problems!' he bellowed, as another thunderous roar snuffed out his voice. There was another flash of light, but this time the crew felt a heavy impact and heard the grind of crunching timber. They realised that it wasn't the storm but an attack from the enemy ship.

'If the storm doesn't smash us apart then that ship surely will,' Rhidian called out. 'What can we do?'

'There's the centre of the storm!' Rebus screeched, pointing ahead. 'Help me steer towards it, Rhidian.' It was their only chance. The *Cloud Hopper* continued to pitch and roll as the attacking vessel collided and then bounced away, only to smash into them once more.

'Hold fast everyone. This is going to be the worst yet,' Rebus called out and sounded a little calmer for some reason. The lightning continued and the thunder followed in deafening bursts as heavy winds and rain added to their devastation. There were a few more shunts from the pirate ship but with the bad conditions they couldn't climb aboard.

'At least the storm is helping us by stopping the pirates!' Rhidian screeched.

The *Cloud Hopper*'s engine wasn't a factor any more as the raging storm took over. Rebus and Rhidian really had no control as they entered oblivion. Red called out from somewhere on the floor.

'The pirate ship has broken off and turned away.' He was right; the captain of that ship had more sense than to pursue something on a death course. The pirate vessel was veering to the left, but, as it peeled away a sharp finger of electrical energy touched down onto its centre, damaging part of the deck. Rhidian could see it free-falling – the balloon that kept it afloat was punctured. Well, that's one problem out of the way, Rhidian thought.

'Hold on, we're not out of the woods yet!' Rebus bellowed.

The rain beat down hard on the ship like stair rods and the wind buffeted the poor vessel from all directions. One great swirl and the *Cloud Hopper* flipped over and was now upside-down. The crew fell and landed against the ceiling. It was dark inside and no one could make out where they were. No one knew if they were all safe. The windows were forced in and shards of glass splintered like diamonds.

Another great fist punched the side of the ship, levelling it back upright. The four figures were thrown back to the floor, the same as dried peas in a rolling can. It was dark and noisy and everyone was disorientated. Thunder erupted and the high tone of the wind made it impossible to hear anything. The cargo ship entered the centre of the squall and twisted like a children's spinning top – round and round it went as the propeller flew off into nothingness.

The small crew were all but unconscious. The engine had cut out when the propeller was ripped away, leaving the ship without power. Then suddenly the violence calmed and gravity took over. With the ship released from the grip of the storm and a huge tear in the canvas that kept in the floating gas, there was nothing to keep it in the air. The vessel picked up speed and plummeted towards whatever lay beneath. Down it fell, occasionally lit by the distant lightning strikes. The rumble of distant thunder seemed to be cursing the ship's escape.

There was still enough ballast in its tanks to keep the *Cloud Hopper* steady and level. And, as it got closer, the parachute automatically released and flowered into a colossal umbrella, slowing down the pace of the ship. It was a controlled decent now rather than an out-of-control rush of speed.

The wooden craft creaked and groaned from its wounds, beaten and helpless, the passengers unaware of anything. The storm drifted and took with it the angry clouds and rasping winds. The rain subsided too, and all that remained were the pale diminishing flashes of lightning and mumbling thunder in the background.

Cloud Hopper was no more and came to land with a resounding thud. It rolled over and lay on its side as if resting. The parachute limply fell, covering its body as a mother pulling a sheet over a baby. The contents of the ship were spread over a mile, leaving the broken shell exposed.

Once more the sun petered through the dissolving cloud cover, penetrating the land with its warm rays, the ship alone in the middle of a desolate land.

Chapter 15
Missing

The ship was mostly whole but looked helpless, like a wounded animal. It lay on its side, grafted to the ground, and appeared as if it had always been there. Debris from the craft were scattered in all directions.

Rhidian was first to open his eyes and found himself upside down. He had bits of wood and other stuff weighing him down. He grunted and slowly moved his head as best as he could. Everything was a haze at first and then the memories of the storm flashed across his mind.

'Oh, man,' he growled from the pit of his throat; his mouth was really dry. He could feel the pressure in his temples and his nose was blocked. He snuffled it up and spit it out. His neck was sore but it didn't give him pain, but he did have a humongous headache. The engineer was afraid to move at first, in case he'd broken something. He plucked up the courage and started to flex his limbs. He could hear and feel pieces of timber and debris drop off him. The blood was pumping in his temples. He eventually righted himself, sat up, and this took the pressure off.

Rhidian had more focus now and saw the mess that was the *Cloud Hopper*. His head felt cloudy and he couldn't think straight at first. He moved his arms and legs but, besides the odd bruise, everything appeared okay. He breathed a sigh of contentment, his head still pounding. The control room was set at an angle. It didn't appear to have sustained too much damage, which struck him as really odd after the wrestle they'd had with the storm. The furniture was obviously all over the place but otherwise fine. He then realised that he was on his own. Where was everyone?

He gently scrambled to his feet. When he stood up straight he had to steady himself against the ceiling (which was now the wall). It took a few more moments before he was ready to move again. He was stood on the starboard side of the ship. The only way out was to climb up to the doorway. He clambered over debris and eventually pulled his body up through the doorframe and onto the deck. From here he could see the full damage to the ship. The day was bright and sunny and he had to shield his eyes from the glare. It was as if everything was normal but everything wasn't. He felt sick from being upside-down and the headache. He needed water.

Rhidian made his way along the port side, using anything he could to help him get a grip. When he'd got to the bow, he could step down onto the sand and walk off the ship. It felt good to be on solid ground again. The engineer walked along the underside of the *Cloud Hopper* and was shocked to find that he was still on his own. Where was everyone? Had they all been scattered over the land? Maybe he was the only one that survived. He was alone and on the brink of crying but choked back the tears. Rhidian wiped his nose and eyes. He had to find the others – they could be hurt, or worse.

He quickly walked back around the ship to look on the deck again and, to his utter joy, found Rebus.

'Good, you're okay,' he said, the relief evident on his face.

'Where's everyone else?' Rebus asked; his voice sounded as dry as Rhidian's.

'I'm here,' Caleb's voice echoed from deep in the galley. He crawled out onto the deck, dragging a container of water behind him.

'Are you all right, Caleb?' Rhidian said urgently, quickly moving to his aid.

'As far as I know,' he replied gingerly. 'Bit sore, but nothing serious. How about you and Rebus?'

'Me, I'm fine. I think Rebus is good too, considering. Can I get a drink?' Rhidian added. 'My mouth doesn't feel part of me at the moment.'

'Sure, give some to Rebus too. He looks as parched as you,' Caleb said. The two men took turns and swallowed hungrily – Rhidian almost choked in the process.

'Take your time, Rhidian. There's plenty in the hold,' Caleb revealed.

'Hey, where's Red?' Rebus piped up. It was at that point that they realised he wasn't there.

'Red? Red, where are you?' Rhidian called out, but an answer didn't come. 'We have to find him.' Rhidian's face was distraught.

'We will,' Caleb cut in. 'He can't be far. I'll check below,' he said, and scrambled along the deck.

'I'll check the cabins,' Rhidian added with purpose.

'I'll look outside the ship in the surrounding area,' Rebus said, and pushed himself along the side of the ship. There was a lot of shouting and creaking timber and, eventually, everyone met on the sandy ground.

'He's not here,' Rebus exclaimed. 'Where the hell is he?'

'Well, we've searched everywhere on board,' Rhidian reported. 'Could he have jumped out maybe? He could be hurt somewhere.'

'He can't be far, surely?' Caleb said, mystified. 'Perhaps he's…'

'Let's not jump to any conclusions,' Rebus cut in smartly.

'Yeah, let's hope he's okay. Anything could have happened in that storm. I'm worried,' Rhidian said.

'Well, what do we do then?' Caleb looked at the others and expected some kind of plan.

'A search party,' Rhidian announced. 'Look, he's a tough kid. I'm sure he's fine,' Rhidian said, and tried to sound upbeat, more for himself than the others.

'Okay, what if we split up and look further afield?' Rebus asked and rolled his eyes from Caleb to Rhidian.

'That makes sense,' Caleb said, and took a look around the ship.

'Before we do anything we have to work out where we are,' Rhidian said sensibly. Rebus and Rhidian did the same as Caleb and scanned the area. They were surrounded by black sand. Rhidian dipped down to the ground and grabbed a handful.

'What is that?' Rebus knelt down by Rhidian's side and fingered the granules in his palm.

'It's obviously sand, but black sand means one thing to me. This whole place must be set on volcanic rock,' Rhidian assumed.

'How do you know that?' Rebus probed.

'I had to learn about rock formation in a course I did years ago,' he said.

'Clever boy,' Rebus said, raising his eyebrows.

'Over here, quickly,' Caleb called from the stern section of the ship. Rebus and Rhidian scampered over the sandy base to meet him.

'What is it?' Rebus gushed.

'I can feel traces of him,' Caleb said seriously.

'What traces?' Rhidian quizzed.

'I have to connect with Rebus and maybe we can find him,' Caleb said.

'Okay, let's do it,' Rebus agreed, eyes wide. The two sorcerers sat down in the sand cross-legged. Rhidian stood back in silence and let them create the magic. Both of them closed their eyes and concentrated. To Rhidian's surprise a plume of smoke conjured from the sand. He gasped and looked on in wonder. Rebus and Caleb were in totally one mind.

Soon the light grey wisp formed into a mirror of sorts and there, in the middle, was a figure. Rhidian recognised it right away; Red was lying on the ground with his eyes shut. Rhidian's heart pounded – was he alive? There was movement and the boy's eyes flickered open. Rhidian couldn't help himself and reached out to touch him. As his finger touched the mist, the apparition dissolved away and the wizards' connection to the boy was broken. Rebus and Caleb opened their eyes, staring at each other.

'Sorry, guys,' Rhidian apologised.

'Sorry?' Caleb looked puzzled. 'Why?'

'I touched the smoke,' Rhidian admitted.

'Don't worry about it,' Rebus said. 'It wouldn't have lasted much longer anyway.'

'We have to find him,' Rhidian said, wringing his hands. 'At least he's alive.' Rhidian's spirits were high again.

'We now know what direction to go to find him,' Caleb said positively.

'We have to go right now,' Rebus added urgently.

'We don't know how far away he is though,' Caleb said and he was right.

'It doesn't matter, he's our friend and we have to help him. We should grab some water and whatever food we have. We've got to go and help the lad,' Rhidian said, his eyes serious.

'You're right, come on. It's a bit of a mess in the kitchen but I'll find something.' Caleb was already climbing back onto the *Cloud Hopper* and within five minutes he returned with a couple of shoulder bags.

'I have water and some fruit. The meat and the rest of the contents in the fridge and freezers are inedible. The power went off and the doors were all open,' Caleb explained.

'That'll keep us going for now. And we've got a direction to follow,' Rhidian chirped up, 'that's something.'

'It's what's we'll find when we get there that I'm not sure of,' Rebus said.

'Whatever it is, we'll deal with it together,' Caleb smiled. And off they went, the strong magic of the wizards leading them.

Chapter 16
Attack

Rhidian took a long look at the landscape before setting off. It looked bleak – the ground was hilly with dips and scars carved into the ground. There were trees dotted here and there, but besides that there was only rock and not much else. It was sunny and the warmth beat down from a bright, yellow sun, but a swift breeze kept the air cool.

He was surprised. The earth was mostly underwater so they must have been lucky enough to land on high ground somewhere. He couldn't make out any stretches of water at all, so he assumed they'd landed deep in the mountains, the problem being that a land shrouded in volcanic rock wouldn't hold much in the way of food.

'Come on, Rhidian, stop pondering and let's get on with it.' Rebus was agitated. They moved off in a northerly direction – the intuition of the wizards leading the way.

'What's up with you?' Rhidian enquired with interest as they strolled along. 'You seem annoyed.'

'Nothing,' he growled and kept his eyes fixed ahead, his heavy sigh obvious.

'He's miffed at the idea of being distracted from searching for Obsidian,' Caleb revealed. Rebus gave Caleb a sharp stare.

'You're not serious?' Rhidian snapped. Rebus' face went from taught and angry to placid. He slowly turned to Rhidian with regret in his eyes.

'I apologise,' he said with real conviction. 'I don't mean to be so self-centred, it's just that… time is running out. We need to find Obsidian and the others as soon as we can. I like Red too, and I'm also worried about him… sorry,' he said.

'One thing at a time, Rebus. Let's get the lad back first, then we have to find transport to take us the rest of the way,' Caleb said, adding to the conversation. They moved over the next hill and Caleb stopped.

'What is it?' Rhidian asked curiously.

'He definitely went this way,' Caleb spoke, peering down the valley.

'Yes, I agree,' Rebus said, adding a nod.

'I can see footprints.' Rhidian raised his voice excitedly. He was right – in the gravel there were impressions.

'Well…' Rebus uttered.

'They're not boots. More like trainers, so it must be Red,' Rhidian gushed. At least the boy was up and walking.

'That's not going to help us much though,' Caleb admitted.

'Why?' Rhidian asked and looked perplexed.

'The ground changes further along,' Rebus cut in. He was right; the shale which they'd been crunching through was soon to change to grass, and that would be more difficult to see where the trail would lead.

'Back to our original plan,' Caleb said.

The three men scrambled their way down the hillside – loose rocks and gravel spilled to the bottom. Rebus slipped and was helped back to his feet by the others. When they got to the treeline the last of the footprints disappeared.

'Where did he go? Is it this way?' Caleb said, flicking his gaze from left to right. He stood with eyes shut, willing his magic to reveal something.

'It's no use, Caleb. I can't feel him either. His essence is fading,' Rebus admitted.

Things were looking grim, until Rhidian knelt down. He ran his eyes along the ground. He paid particular attention to the grass and shrubs. The three of them were in a clearing and the sun shone through the overhanging branches, leaving bright, luminous shapes on the grass. The continuing winds made the tree limbs tremble, making it seem as though the trees were whispering to each other.

'Well?' Rebus croaked impatiently. Rhidian said nothing for a moment and looked straight ahead.

'Ah hah,' he finally chirped up. 'The grass is flattened and these shrubs have been disturbed. That wide gap between the trees is where I think he must have gone.' Rhidian looked up at his two wizard companions, a smile beamed all over his face. Wizard intuition, he thought... pah!

'All right then, we go that way.' Caleb walked off and left the others in his wake.

'Hold on, Caleb,' Rebus called after him. 'We have to be vigilant. I feel we're getting really close. We don't know if there's anything else here.'

'Stop!' Rhidian shouted.

'What...?' But Rebus didn't have time to continue.

'Shhh!' Rhidian had his finger to his lips. 'Listen.'

By this time Caleb had returned. He looked blankly at Rebus who looked just as mystified at Rhidian. Then it happened. The sound of a low-pitched growl that rumbled along the ground and vibrated up through their bodies. Everyone froze.

'What is that?' Caleb mouthed the words. Rebus and Rhidian shook their heads, mystified. All three of them dipped down behind a small clump of bushes. The clearing turned into centre stage and the biggest bear anyone had ever seen now occupied it. It was six feet on all fours, so Rebus calculated it would reach at least twelve feet when fully upright. Caleb's eyes resembled giant rock pools. Rhidian's bottom jaw dropped so low that he almost rubbed his chin on the ground.

The bear was humongous, its paws easily the size of a large dinner plate. It snuffled the grass with its wet, black, shiny snout and lifted its head up, sniffing the air. Rhidian held his breath. The animal must have recognised the odour. It immediately opened its gaping mouth and let out a colossal growl and revealed a row of huge front canines, jagged and sharp as rocks. The ground physically shook as if frightened by this monstrous beast. The sound was deafening making the three men wince. The bear looked in their direction and they knew the game was up.

'What do we do?' Rhidian whispered in terror, his eyes almost popped out of his head.

'There's not a lot we can do,' Caleb responded.

'He's right. We have to face this thing,' Rebus said reluctantly.

'FACE IT?' Rhidian gushed. There was another loud roar, as if the bear was inviting them to reveal themselves. All three stepped from behind the bush, fully knowing they didn't have a chance to outrun the animal. Upon seeing them, the monster let out another huge snarl. Rhidian trembled so much he didn't know if he could hold himself up. He switched his gaze from Rebus to Caleb… they appeared calm. How did they do that when he felt as though he was about to throw up?

'What… are… we… going… to… do?' Rhidian said, and barely got the words out.

'Caleb,' Rebus said, and quickly whispered into his ear. Caleb nodded in agreement.

'Whatever you're going to do, guys, do it now,' Rhidian squeaked.

The huge bear was about to strike and lowered its head to the ground. It let out the biggest and longest roar Rhidian had ever heard. Everything within a mile shook as if hit by a massive explosion. Its mouth was wide open and inside revealed the most powerful set of jaws. Rhidian could see quite clearly deep scars of battle gouged into its fur. This beast was no stranger to a fight and would make mincemeat of them in no time.

If the roar wasn't an impressive enough show of dominance, then the next thing that happened took their breath away… it stood up! The three men took a step back and each craned their necks to take in the enormity of its size. This animal was colossal – at least twelve feet tall at its peak. It would need heavy weaponry just to slow it down.

'Oh, GOD, we're all going to die!' Rhidian said, the words falling from his gaping mouth. The engineer had forgotten his quest. Nothing mattered to him now but how violently he was going to part this world. He could feel warm tears welling up in the corner of his eyes and his nose began to stream.

He found himself taking short, sharp breaths but panic was just another element of fear.

Another almighty roar suddenly filled the air and Rhidian turned his head with a jerk to see what was happening. He couldn't believe it – another bear appeared from a gap in the rocks. This one was brown and just as big and powerful as the black one. The second bear slowly padded towards the black bear and a battle was about to commence.

Rhidian took a few steps back and collided with a tree, which instantly winded him. He looked on, knowing there was nothing he could do to defend himself against these huge beasts. He noticed though that the black bear looked confused. Rhidian was still trying to breathe as he studied the other animal. He noticed too, that it looked very similar to the black bear. Not only that, but it had identical scarring as the other bear. He gasped for air, but he also couldn't work out what was going on. The brown bear then let out another howl that overshadowed the black bear's dominant call. This really shook old black's confidence.

Soon everyone could see that there was a definite change in the situation. The black bear suddenly began to cower – its ears drooped and so did its shoulders. Rhidian glanced over to Caleb and Rebus who were fully concentrating on some spell or something. They were standing each side of the brown bear and had both eyes closed. Rhidian was overwhelmed.

These two bears were more than he could handle. Had the wizards combined magic to conjure up this apparition? Was it real, or was it just coincidence? Rhidian was taking no chances and flattened himself against the tree as much as he could. He closed his eyes and clenched his mouth shut.

The brown bear let out another colossal roar and that was enough to secure the situation. The first bear looked broken and dropped down onto all fours. The next thing, it let out a couple of high-pitched whimpers, then backed away. Rhidian opened his eyes a crack... and then fully. The two sorcerers were still fully committed to their illusion and didn't move. The black bear was no more and scampered off beyond the trees, with the brown bear still bellowing in its wake.

'Okay, fellas... it's gone!' Rhidian shouted. The bear turned to him and leaned forward and bared its teeth. Rhidian screamed and threw his arms up to protect himself. And then silence. Rhidian slowly dropped his hands down when he heard the sound of chuckling and was confronted by two grinning wizards. The engineer stared back, eyes blazing. Then, he relented and shook his head.

'You...'

'Now, now, Rhidian, there's no need for any ill will,' Rebus said, still beaming. Caleb's grin was so wide that Rhidian thought the top of his head would fall off.

'How on earth did you manage that?' he asked, still physically shaking from the trauma.

'You'd have to be a wizard to know that, my friend,' Caleb responded. 'The main thing is it worked.'

'That could have gone so wrong,' Rhidian expressed.

'Did you have any other ideas?' Rebus said, scornfully.

'No, I guess not, and I am grateful, but we still have to find Red,' he insisted.

'True, and time is of the essence. There is a wild bear out here and Red is on his own. He wouldn't stand a chance against that thing and I don't know if that spell would work again,' Caleb admitted.

'OK, I can still see where the ground has been disturbed. Let's just hope it's Red that has disturbed it.'

'Let's go then, guys, but keep an eye out for Barney,' Rebus joked.

'Barney? Are you serious? It's got to be Jeremy,' Caleb added.

'Shut up, guys,' Rhidian said, still feeling a little bruised from the joke they'd pulled.

Soon they disappeared into the thicket and resumed the search for Red.

'GRRRRRR!' Rebus growled.

'Not funny, Rebus,' Rhidian snapped back.

'It kind of is though,' Caleb joined in.

'Right, that's enough,' Rhidian continued, and after one or two more growls, Caleb and Rebus relented.

Chapter 17
Imago Pirates

The tracks continued for a while and then disappeared again. They all stopped and stared at the ground. Rebus spoke up.

'What do we do now?' he asked, looking concerned. 'We've no trail to follow.'

'I don't know, but we can't give up.' Rhidian was worried but adamant about continuing the search.

'I understand you're concerned about young Red, but the light is fading and I've lost his essence,' Caleb said, pointing above.

Night was indeed slowly devouring the blue sky, adding a deep purple to the backdrop. The trees were fanned out, but the twilight still hid them from predators. The urgency of finding their friend, and the inevitability of darkness, made Caleb, Rebus and Rhidian forge on in silence and only spoke when they needed to. As it got darker, movement became more difficult.

'Did anyone think to bring a flashlight?' Rhidian said, realising he hadn't.

'Didn't you?' Rebus said, and tried to look into Rhidian's eyes but it was too dark.

'No I didn't. I thought you did,' Rhidian responded.

'What about you, Caleb?' Rebus asked.

'Me, no, I was too busy getting the food,' he answered.

'So... none of us thought to bring a light?' Rebus said with a sigh. There were shakes of the head all around, 'I suppose things were a bit crazy back there.'

'Hold up a sec,' Caleb said and dipped to the ground.

'What is it?' Rhidian was feeling excited. 'You found his trail again?' he asked, his voice sounding upbeat.

'No, just grabbing a tree branch,' Caleb revealed. Rhidian couldn't quite see what he was doing as the night had smothered everything and made it difficult to see anything. 'I'm going to try and make a burning torch,' Caleb said. 'We'll need light.'

'We're going to have to stop soon anyway, light or no light,' Rebus grumbled. 'It's getting too dangerous.' He was right of course, but Rhidian didn't want to give up.

'Just a little further,' Rhidian chirped up, hoping the rest would agree. 'Please, I'm really worried about Red.'

Caleb had found some small rocks and emptied one of the food bags into the other. He wrapped the canvas bag around the top of the branch and tied it as tight as he could to the wood. He used the straps to secure it. He smashed the rocks together and produced sparks. Soon a small flame appeared, catching the fibres of the dry cloth.

'We have light,' Caleb announced proudly, but that was short lived. 'Look, there,' he said urgently. He pointed the flame towards something, not too far ahead. There were also lights in the distance. All three were astounded.

'Where did they come from?' Rhidian asked. 'I didn't notice them before.'

'We weren't concentrating and we're tired,' Rebus exclaimed.

'An encampment?' Rhidian whispered. 'Could be trouble. Do you think it's Red?'

'We have to get a closer look without being seen. Then we can see what it's all about,' Rebus replied.

'Yeah, everyone keep their eyes peeled,' Caleb instructed.

'You're going to have to put out that torch,' Rebus insisted. 'That'll give us away before we get anywhere near.' There was a huge sigh from Caleb.

'I've only just lit this,' he groaned, but he understood and stubbed it out in the mud, but kept hold of the stick just in case he needed it for a weapon.

They scrambled along the ground – it was slow going, but the lights in the distance were getting brighter.

'This is hopeless,' Rhidian groaned.

'Stop complaining. You were the one who wanted to keep going,' Rebus rasped.

'We can climb up here and maybe see what's going on,' Caleb cut in, and was already making his way to the top of a grassy knoll. Rebus and Rhidian scrambled up behind him, huffing and puffing as they went. The three men slithered along the ground like snipers and peered over a small stump. The lights in the distance reflected in their eyes.

'Can you make anything out at all?' Rebus whispered into Caleb's ear, his tired eyes squinting, not as true as they once were. Ahead was what looked like a makeshift camping site. It looked empty of any people, but someone must have lit the torches.

'I can't see movement beyond the fires, but from here it looks like some kind of entrance,' Caleb admitted.

'We have to get a closer look,' Rhidian whispered, his determination building.

'Okay, but everyone keep your heads down,' Rebus insisted.

They got to their feet, but bent themselves double in order not to be seen. The night sky was shrouded in grey clouds, with no sign of a moon. They kept well hidden and, as they moved in, found a formation of boulders metres from the entrance and ducked down behind them. They were close enough now to see everything. The area was totally exposed by the yellow flames. There were four stakes planted in the ground, set outside the entrance to a cave.

'What is this all about?' Rhidian was unable to work it out. 'Do you think Red has gone in there?' he asked Rebus.

'I don't know,' Rebus replied, rubbing his beard. 'I'm picking up something, but not sure if it's him,' he said honestly.

'Maybe it's just a deterrent,' Caleb said.

'What do you mean?' Rhidian asked, 'a deterrent for what?'

'Well, perhaps it's just to keep away any animals, like that bear we encountered,' Caleb continued. 'Maybe no one ever comes here and whoever is in there doesn't need to worry about being attacked.'

'Well, there's only one way to find out, especially if Red is in there,' Rebus said.

'Maybe only one of us should go in and see if it's safe,' Caleb said, and peered at his two friends in the pale light from the cave.

'Makes sense to me,' Rebus agreed.

'Who's going in then?' Rhidian asked.

'I'll do it and I'll signal you to come in if it's safe,' Caleb assured them.

'Are you sure, Caleb? I don't mind doing it,' Rhidian commented.

'It's fine, honestly.' With that, he got up and looked all around before he made his way to the mouth of the cave. The light from the flames exposed him fully to anything that lay inside. So, instead of gingerly edging forward, he simply walked in and disappeared into the shadows.

It was blindingly dark inside the entrance, worse than the forest. So black in fact, that he had to grope more than walk along the passageway. The surface of the wall was coarse and felt like a really abrasive sponge. He moved slowly and deliberately; there might be hidden dangers, he figured. He didn't need to injure himself at this stage. To his utter delight after only minutes of edging forward, there was safety in a small source of light. It was only a pale glow, but was enough for him to get his bearings. The closer he got, the brighter the beam became. The lighted torch revealed the entrance of an inner cave. With the light came signs of life and a smattering of muted conversations, which echoed from within. Caleb immediately ducked out of sight and held his breath. There were people here.

The voices amplified from further within. Caleb kept his back flattened as best he could to the cave wall and engaged the light. The voices were, in fact, further away than he realised, and he felt more confident that they wouldn't see him. This section of the cave was a lot narrower, and he had to turn sideways to fit through. It was instantly brighter in here and now he felt really exposed. Caleb dipped down to his left where there was cover. He squatted until he felt confident enough to lift himself to look over the top.

He very slowly put his hands on the boulder he was hiding behind and eased up to eye-level. The wizard couldn't believe what he witnessed. Way in the background there was a lot of activity.

'Good grief… the ship!' Caleb gasped. He looked on in amazement. The pirate ship that had been following them through the storm was right there. He squinted to try and see what they were doing. They were repairing it. Of course, he thought, Rhidian had said something about them breaking away from pursuing them.

'Come on, you lot, I want this repaired by morning. We have to get after that cargo ship.' There was a big overbearing character on the deck, out of focus for Caleb to get any real detail. He was bellowing orders and Caleb presumed he was the captain. There was a crew of about ten that he could make out in the semi-light. The ship was nestled on a jetty and tethered by two ropes. It was a fine vessel. It had a huge balloon above it that gave the whole thing lift. Also, it was made in the shape of an old galleon from centuries ago.

'That's it, men, almost finished. Good job fixing the balloon. There'll be plenty to drink after you complete the job… NOW GET ON WITH IT!' he bellowed; his voice boomed through the tunnels. The crew seemed to jerk back in fear. This captain was a heavy presence.

Caleb took a look around and noticed that things were stacked near to him. There were supplies on the jetty waiting to be put on board. Further back again was a fire set on a plinth of a flat rock, which had been hewn into shape by time. This must be where they enjoy a drink and relax, Caleb surmised.

Suddenly something else caught his eye. There was movement from the rocks further back – a figure that could not be seen by the thieving crew. And Caleb recognised him straight away… it was Red. He needed to get his attention but didn't want to give away his own position and let the captain know he was being spied on.

Red seemed to look beyond the pirates to a place high up on the rocks. There was a cage of sorts set on a ledge. Caleb could just about make out what was inside. It looked like a man, huddled up in the back. What was Red going to do? He would surely get himself caught if he tried to rescue him. Caleb had to get his attention. The wizard searched around the ground and found some pebbles by his feet. He picked up two – they were each about the size of a grape.

He weighed one up in his hand, aimed and tossed it towards Red's direction. It cracked against the boulder just behind him and bounced out of sight. Red immediately ducked and hid. The pirates were unconcerned by the sound; they'd probably heard the sounds of the cave a million times. Caleb was just about to throw another when Red popped his head up. The boy saw Caleb and a big smile beamed on his face. He put his finger urgently to his lips for Red to keep quiet. He motioned with a wave of his hand for Red to join him. Red understood and kept himself below the height of the rocks and scrambled to where Caleb was waiting. Red hugged Caleb as if he hadn't seen him for years.

'The others are outside. Are you all right?' Red nodded vigorously. 'Right, follow me.'

'What about the prisoner?' Red looked really concerned. He recalled the day he'd been taken to Skytraz; it stuck to his memory like mud on a blanket. 'We can't just leave him there to die. We have to break him out,' the boy insisted with deep concern.

'We can't do anything at this moment, Red. We have to work out what we've got to do. Come on, let's go back to the others and build a plan,' Caleb said, and the two of them made their way back outside to the delight of Rhidian and Rebus.

Chapter 18
Skyward

They were soon all together once more and even Rebus looked pleased to see the young lad.

'You all right, Red?' Rhidian asked after he'd hugged him. 'You scared us, lad.'

'Here.' Rebus held out a bottle of water and Red grabbed and swallowed hard.

'Take it easy, boy, we don't have much left,' Caleb said. After he'd had a drink, Rebus gave him an apple.

'What happened? How did you get here?' Rhidian was intrigued to know.

'All I remember,' he said as he took a couple of breaths in between chomping on the fruit, 'is falling off our ship and landing in the sea.'

'How did you manage?' Caleb probed.

'I was so shocked at hitting the cold water that I swam as best as I could to the shoreline.' Red took another bite out of the apple.

'It was dark though. How did you know where the shore was?' Rebus interjected.

'I don't know, I just swam and the next thing I knew I was lying on dry ground,' Red recalled.

'It must have been further down the mountain. What happened next, Red?' Rhidian pressed. All three of them stood listening to his tale.

'I got up and walked through the trees until I eventually found a stream,' he said. 'I drank some water and heard voices.'

'And then, what next?' the interrogation from the men continued. Red didn't speak for a moment or two while he swallowed the last of the apple.

'I was going to show myself and ask for help, but I heard one of them mention our ship and that scared me.' Red said, his expression intense.

'What did they say?' Rhidian asked, totally engrossed with the conversation.

'Well, one voice said that Captain Jacobs couldn't wait to get us and rob us of our supplies. But they needed to repair their ship first. Then someone else said Captain Jacobs was going to kill all the crew once they did catch up with us.' Red looked nervous as he spoke.

'What are we going to do?' Rhidian was the first to put the question forward.

'Our ship is damaged beyond repair,' Caleb said truthfully.

'We have to take theirs.' Rebus said the words and looked through to them.

'Wh-at?' Red's face went pale.

'That's going to take some doing, Rebus,' Caleb said and licked his lips.

'How many are there?' Rhidian asked.

'At least ten,' Caleb and Red said in unison.

'B-but, what about the prisoner?' Red stammered.

'Prisoner? What prisoner?' Rebus questioned. 'No one mentioned anything about a prisoner.'

'There's someone locked up in a cage in there too,' Caleb revealed sheepishly. 'Sorry, I forgot to say. I couldn't make out if it was a man or a woman. The poor thing was cowering right at the back.'

'We can't worry about anyone else. We have to get that ship as quickly as we can and get out of this place,' Rebus grunted. 'If we try and do a rescue mission, it could jeopardise our own escape.'

'We have to help whoever is in there,' Red pleaded. 'You can't leave someone to die.'

'Hold on, are we doing this tonight?' Rhidian cut in. Caleb looked serious and tired.

'The captain said they had to get the ship ready for the morning. And I think it was almost completed. The only chance we have is to take it tonight. Once they've filled themselves with whisky, they'll fall asleep and we can have the upper hand. If we don't, they're bound to find our ship once they're in the air. Then,' he paused, 'they'll eventually find us,' Caleb said.

'We'll need a plan then,' Rhidian interjected, scratching his head.

'The plan is we go back inside, hide and strike when they're sleeping, like Caleb said,' Rebus repeated.

'What about the prisoner?' Red pressed.

'We'll see what we can do, but no promises,' Rebus continued, feeling disillusioned by the whole thing. Time was wasting and they still weren't anywhere near finding Obsidian.

'We may have to take the prisoner with us,' Rhidian continued. 'If whoever is in there sees us leaving without them, they might raise the alarm.' Rebus creased up his face and then pondered the situation for a moment.

'You might be right, Rhidian. Red, we'll rescue your friend, but we don't even know why that prisoner has been locked up. Maybe he or she is a murderer?' Rebus exclaimed.

'I doubt it. They're probably the murderers, that person is just an innocent victim, like us,' Red said.

'Enough talking, we have to go and hide inside, otherwise our chance maybe lost,' Caleb said with authority. They all agreed – it was a plan. Caleb led the way and the others followed behind, groping in the dark again. By the time they'd entered the second cave, the pirates were already sitting around the fire, laughing and drinking. One or two were even squabbling amongst themselves.

Caleb and the others filed in one-by-one and hid in the same place that he'd done when he first went inside. They settled there for what felt like hours – waiting – waiting – waiting. Cramp set in on Red's leg and he almost screamed out in pain. It was only when Rhidian stretched his leg out and Caleb clamped a hand over his mouth that the cramps subsided and Red relaxed. The rowdy crewmen eventually burned themselves out and the howls diminished into rattled snoring and farting, which echoed throughout the cave.

'It's time,' Caleb whispered and Rebus nodded. Red and Rhidian's nerves were on edge; they hated the idea, but there was no other way. The engineer looked at Red, who tentatively peered back and rolled his eyes. The lights had mostly dimmed and the roaring fire had burned down to a yellow-blue glow. It sparked and spat the sap from the remains of the scorched wood that settled in the embers.

'Are they all by the fire?' Caleb whispered as they stood up.

'Shhh, there's no knowing,' Rebus hissed back.

The four of them quietly walked past the sleeping bodies and towards the boat. There were a couple of low burning oil lamps that offered a dim view of the scene. Red looked up and saw that it actually *was* a man in the cage. He moved towards the bars and signalled to Red with a wave of his hand. Red tugged at Caleb's shirt and pointed towards the figure.

'He can see us,' he gushed. The man was more of a silhouette but was definitely pointing to something. There glinting on a nail was a key.

By now, Rebus and Rhidian had walked along the gangplank and were boarding the ship. Rhidian looked up and the balloon was fully gassed up. Last time he had seen it, it was punctured.

'Do you think you can run this thing?' Rebus spoke quietly.

'I think so. We'll have to do the same as we did at Skytraz Prison – float away quietly at first, then start the motor,' Rhidian said as he made his way to the navigation room. There was no one on board the ship, to everyone's relief. Why would there be? Rhidian thought. They were inside a secret cave – *he* and the wizards had only come across it by accident.

'Caleb, we have to help him,' Red insisted, and craned his neck to look again at the prisoner.

'All right, I'll come with you,' Caleb agreed, 'but we have to be quick. We could be found out at any moment.' They walked past the sleeping crew again and climbed to the top.

'Get the keys,' Caleb whispered. The wizard edged closer to the enclosure and looked at the man inside. He couldn't make out much, but what he could see was a thin-framed body with sad eyes staring back.

'Please help me,' he squeaked in a dry voice. Red hurriedly clambered up to the key and snatched it off the nail. But he didn't grasp the ring properly, and it slipped from his hand. The key dropped to the ground and the tinkling sound rang out a warning. Caleb urgently looked at Red, gritted his teeth and dived down behind the cage. Red flattened himself to the ground as best he could. Both Rebus and Rhidian realised what had happened and hid on the deck. The prisoner eased back into the shadows of his cage.

Two pirates blinked open their eyes and sat up. They looked around the cave – they were still half asleep. A wry smile came to one when he saw a quarter bottle of rum on its side next to him. He grabbed it and swallowed. The other snatched it off him and sunk the dregs. They both slumped back into a drunken coma.

The raiding party surfaced again. Rebus and Rhidian worked on the ship and Red got back up and sheepishly approached Caleb, who was looking at him with unblinking eyes. He handed him the keys and the prisoner waited in anticipation. Caleb toyed with the lock – there were a couple of blunt clicks until it released. As quietly and slowly as possible, he pulled gently on the iron door. It let out a slow, high-pitched yawn, but to everyone's surprise it didn't wake any of the crew. At last the man was released. He stepped out and shakily straightened himself up. He was thin and dirty. He let out a huge stretch, as if he'd been in a cramped position for a long time.

'Are you coming with us?' Caleb asked.

'Yes, please,' he replied politely, his voice hollow.

'Come on,' Red and Caleb said, and carefully led him to the ship. Soon they were all on board and furiously worked to get the vessel unhitched from dock.

'Pull in the gangplank and release the ropes,' Rebus ordered in a high-pitched whisper. Red and Caleb pulled in the long wooden plank and threw off the thick tethers that held the ship in place. Soon the vessel began to rise. The ship, though, jerked and was yanked back towards the jetty. It hit the side with a clang that shook the whole wooden structure. The sound and vibration was enough to wake anything asleep or dead.

'What's happening?' Rebus screeched, not caring to whisper any more; it was too late for that. The pirates were shaken from sleep and trying to work out what was happening. Red noticed a rope that they'd missed, still attached to the stern.

'There, look, I'll get it!' Red screamed.

'Release it now!' Rebus bellowed. Red ran over to try and unloop it, but the ship was pulling away again and the rope was taut. The pirates were on their feet now and grappling for their weapons.

'I c-can't – it's too tight,' Red screeched, straining. Caleb raced over to give him a hand. Shots were fired and bullets ricocheted, taking small chunks out of the ship's timbers. The boy and the wizard frantically tugged at the rope, but it was no use as the ship again was yanked back. Bullets were thick and fast coming from all directions.

'Release the bloody rope,' Rebus cursed. 'HURRY!'

Caleb and Red saw their chance when the rope went slack for a few seconds. They pounced and lifted it over the metal hook. The ship was free again and began to float skywards.

Rhidian and Rebus were at the control panel. The room itself was bigger than the *Cloud Hopper* and surprisingly clean. There were the usual knobs and dials and Rhidian found the starter.

'Let's get out of here!' Rhidian shouted urgently.

'Start her up!' Rebus screamed. Rhidian did as he was told and the engine, to their delight, burst into life first time of asking. The propeller started to spin and when Rhidian pushed the throttle forward it picked up speed. Two pirates managed to run and jump on the ship – a third tried the same and missed. He fell and the scream eventually faded to nothing.

The prisoner, Caleb and Red were the only ones left to defend the ship. The pirates rushed at them, armed with daggers.

'Get back, Red, I'll deal with this,' Caleb commanded. He lifted his arms and showed the attackers his palms. He whispered something as they approached. Red and the stranger noticed that a light had formed in his hands. There was a burst of energy from the wizard and the two pirates were propelled straight over the side, and into oblivion.

'Everybody get down,' Rebus shouted, as the bullets flew from below – some lodged into the timbers but had a stray bullet pierced the balloon? The sudden thrust of the engine allowed the vessel to lift at speed high into the sky. The sounds of gunfire quickly diminished as the ship finally floated out of range. They were free!

Chapter 19
Slipstream

'Is there any damage to the balloon?' Rebus called out as he exited the control room, concern etched on his face. Red and Caleb craned their necks to examine the material as best as they could. There were lights to help them. There was also an array of lamps all along the sides of the vessel. They checked around the whole thing.

'It's still fully inflated,' Red shouted from the stern, 'as far as I can see. I assume it would already start to deflate if there was a puncture and we would be free-falling.'

'Yes, it looks fine this end, too.' Caleb was at the bow and scrutinised every angle, 'I can't see any of the material losing shape,' he said.

'It looks good here, too,' the timid voice of the stranger called from the centre of the deck.

'Phew, that was close,' Rebus gasped, and leaned over the side and looked down at the pinpricks of diminishing light. 'That could have been a disaster,' he mumbled.

'It very nearly was,' Red whispered to himself, with the key drop incident still fresh in his mind.

'Everything is fine,' Caleb relayed to Rhidian, as he walked into the navigation room. Rhidian felt relieved, and as the vessel rose higher it lifted out of the cave opening and the engineer steered it to their original course.

'Would you like to wash and get some clean clothes?' Red asked the stranger as they stood on deck. The old man looked pathetic – skinny, dirty and tired.

'Oh, yes, please,' he answered gratefully.

'I'm sure there should be something on board to suit you. We'll take a look below,' Red said, and led the way. 'Follow me.' The old man took a couple of steps and wobbled. Red turned and saw this, then quickly moved to his side to help. 'Come on, we'll take our time.'

'Where you going?' Rebus called after them as he, too, joined Rhidian and Caleb.

'To get some clothes and stuff.' Red shouted before he and the stranger disappeared below deck.

A little while later, Red and the man entered the control room – soon Red was gone again. The chitchat from Rhidian, Caleb and Rebus stopped abruptly. Rebus peered at the stranger.

'Alba, is that you?' Rebus said and looked totally shocked.

'Yes, Rebus, it is,' Alba retorted when he realised it was his old friend, and the both of them embraced.

'You two know each other, I gather?' Rhidian was intrigued.

'He's a wizard,' Caleb cut in. 'I felt it when he stepped out of the cage.'

'Yes, I'm one of the wizards that escaped Valusha,' Alba revealed, breaking away from the embrace.

'Me, too, but I don't think we've ever met,' Caleb said.

'There were a few of us,' Alba responded with a shake of his head.

'You look a little… tired,' Rebus commented. 'You're getting old,' he quipped, a smile curving his mouth.

'Being locked up and not getting much sleep or much to eat or drink, will do that to you,' Alba responded dryly.

'How *did* you get mixed up with those villains?' Rhidian enquired, keen to get to know their new friend.

'I used all my magic steering a small vessel from Valusha. Everyone else had gone – escaped or otherwise,' he said. 'Those pirates,' he gritted his teeth as he spoke, 'they picked me up while I was drifting. I was weak from hunger and thirst.

Their intention was to get the reward money offered for me.'

There were raised eyebrows and Alba picked up on this. 'Jenta-Lor is offering large amounts of cash to whoever can bring back any wizards that escaped. Captain Jacobs was going to drop me off, when they were next in the area. They were crafty. They kept me weak so I couldn't build my magic… I hate pirates.' His steely glare gave away the fire he felt inside.

'Well, you're here now and, once we find Obsidian and take over Valusha again, things will get better,' Rebus said with determination.

'You're looking for *Obsidian*?' The old wizard looked surprised. 'Do you think he'll want to go back after how they treated him?' Alba asked.

Rebus looked into Alba's eyes… unblinking. 'The people know they made a mistake by electing Jenta-Lor to rule in the first place. I think they want Obsidian back desperately. As much as we do,' Rebus concluded. Life is not good for the people of Valusha at present.

Red entered the room with food supplies.

'The galley is full to bursting,' he said cheerfully, still chewing on something.

'Well done, lad, you're learning,' Caleb said, shaking his head in disbelief.

'Where is Obsidian?' Alba interrupted.

'We think he's in Gelbar and that's where we're headed,' Rebus informed. 'Come on, let's eat, everyone. We've got a journey where we need our wits and strength about us,' Rebus said.

'What's happening Rhidian?' Caleb asked, his eyes narrowing. 'You look agitated.' And the wizard walked over to the control panel. Rhidian was looking intently at the instruments.

'There's something wrong,' he said. 'The fuel dial is dropping.' As he said it, the engine faltered and cut out. Red stopped what he was doing, fear ripping through his body. He looked at Caleb.

'I wondered why they weren't aiming at the balloon,' Celeb remembered.

'What do you mean?' Rebus asked with trepidation.

'I'll let you know in a minute. Rhidian, come with me,' Caleb urged, and waved his hand for Rhidian to follow him. They hurried along the deck and down below. When they got there they could smell the damage.

'They weren't aiming at the balloon, were they? I'll bet the captain didn't want to damage the ship.' Rhidian was shaking his head.

'Yeah, they were aiming at the fuel tank. They knew where it was situated, and also knew it would cripple us. If they can get our ship up and running they'll soon be after us,' Caleb said gravely.

'Our ship was completely wrecked. They won't be repairing that in a hurry,' Rhidian added, knowing how much work was involved.

'I can't do anything with *this* ship without the proper materials,' Rhidian admitted, 'and fuel,' he added.

'They were probably going to load them in the morning,' Caleb surmised. The ship listed and the two men immediately had to grab hold of the something to keep upright.

'What's happening now?' Rhidian gasped.

'Let's get up top and hope Captain Jacobs hasn't caught up with us already,' Caleb hissed, his eyes filled with discontent. The two men rushed up onto the deck and were met with a strong wind buffering the ship. They clambered along the wooden floor, trying to keep balance. When they got to the navigation room, everyone was inside waiting for them.

'What do we do?' Rebus said.

'I think we've hit a slipstream. We've no control in here. There's nothing we can do, only ride it out,' Rhidian assumed. 'We can't pull away from this, it's too strong and we've already lost all our fuel. The balloon is fully inflated but with no power it will take us where it wants. Hold on.'

'You heard Rhidian, everyone hold onto something solid,' Caleb said as the ship tilted even more. The winds picked up speed and tossed the ship from side to side. The small crew held on inside the control room, hoping it would soon blow itself out.

'We haven't had much luck since we left the prison, have we?' Red cringed at what he'd just said. He'd rather be in a storm than back in that jail, though.

'I can try and hold a steady course,' Rhidian bellowed. 'Can't you keep it steady with magic?'

'We'll try,' Rebus said. 'Alba, have you enough strength to help us? With just a small amount of magic it could make all the difference,' he insisted.

'I'll try,' Alba replied and still looked very weak.

'That's all I ask,' Rebus added.

All three wizards, Rebus, Caleb and Alba, sat on the cabin floor and closed their eyes. Rhidian or Red couldn't see what they were doing, but after a short while the ship began to settle and kept a smoother course. There was relief as things calmed. The ripping slipstream threw everything at them, but after an hour, the wind died down and the wizards broke free from their spell.

'There's land!' Red shouted from the deck and ran to help Alba, who looked as if he was going to collapse. The clouds were almost clear and a dense wooded landscape revealed itself. 'Maybe there's fuel down there?'

'I'm going to try and set down while we've still got buoyancy,' Rhidian said. 'Everyone agree?' There was a reluctant nod from everyone but they all knew there really wasn't much choice.

'I'll let the gas out of the balloon,' Caleb said and went outside. There was a release valve with a rope hanging from it. This must let the gas from the balloon and the ship should soon lose altitude, he assumed.

'Not too much, Caleb!' Rhidian shouted from the wheel. 'Gently, little-by-little. We don't want to crash land.' Rhidian kept the pirate ship steady as they dropped from the calm blue sky. Caleb released small amounts of gas that hissed when the valve opened and Rhidian steered towards a patch of open ground. Down and down the craft drifted until it landed with a thump. Rhidian had navigated the ship so that it rested against the treeline and kept upright.

The great balloon looked more like a mutilated melon as it slowly flopped to one side and dragged the ropes with it.

'Don't empty it completely, Caleb,' Rhidian urged, thinking ahead. 'We may need a quick getaway and we can re-inflate it later.'

'But we won't be able to fly it without fuel,' Red said with confusion.

'True,' Rhidian said, 'but once we're up in the air at least we'll be out of harm's way. I can figure out how to repair the tank and if we find some oil we can get it going again later.' Red nodded in compliance.

'Let's tie it down then,' Caleb said. 'If we fix the rope to those trees we can free it later.'

'Good thinking,' Rhidian said in praise.

'Not only engineers have good ideas,' Caleb replied with a wink and a sly grin. 'Come on, you lot, give us a hand.'

'What happens now?' Rhidian looked at Rebus.

'We have to find out where we are first,' he retorted dryly. 'Okay, gather round everyone. We need a plan,' Rebus insisted.

Chapter 20
Sacred Ground

Oak trees surrounded them and it was so dense that it was almost impossible to get a bearing to find out their position.

'I haven't seen this much greenery in a long, long time,' Rhidian admitted and snuffled in the fragrance of the leaves. He closed his eyes – it was amazing.

'Me, neither,' Red agreed, and ran his hands along the rough bark of the closest tree.

'We must be at a high altitude,' Rhidian assumed. Red just shrugged his shoulder.

'I think we're in *Gelbar*,' Rebus announced with great enthusiasm.

'I think you're right,' Alba assured him.

'Gelbar. So we're here,' Red said with a hint of excitement.

'How do you know?' Rhidian pressed. 'There are trees everywhere around here. It's impossible to see anything.'

'I know what you're saying, Rhidian, but I recognise this place.' Rebus seemed convinced.

'Alba?' Rhidian said.

'I'm getting the same feeling – don't ask me why,' he said.

'We have to find higher ground where we can work out exactly which way to go.' Rhidian was looking a little panicked, and felt hemmed in. It was claustrophobic to say the least. Before they could move out, Rebus stopped, said nothing and closed his eyes. Red looked at him with concern.

'You all right, Rebus?' Red asked.

'Hold on, Red, don't touch him,' Rhidian said. 'Look at the others.' He'd noticed that Caleb and Alba were also standing quietly with eyes closed. 'They're experiencing something that only sorcerers can.' Rhidian was right and all three wizards were homing in on some kind of signal. Red sat down on the ground – he felt a little giddy.

'Are you all right, Red? Do you want some water?' Rhidian asked and touched his shoulder for support.

'Y-es please,' Red stammered. 'I-I don't know what's come over me.' Rhidian handed him a bottle and Red gulped it down.

'You'll be all right. Just sit there for a moment. This place is very dense and can suck the air out of your lungs,' Rhidian added.

'He's here, somewhere,' Caleb opened his eyes and spoke.

'Yes – yes, he's definitely here,' Rebus said, revealing the biggest smile.

'I haven't felt that kind of feeling in a long while… since Valusha,' Alba gushed.

'How far away is he?' Red questioned and didn't look as flushed.

'Can't tell for certain, but I think it's this way,' Rebus said and pointed to a small opening in the trees. 'One thing I do know is that *he* doesn't know we're here. I didn't get anything back from him.' Rebus looked disappointed. The other wizards nodded in agreement.

'Maybe he doesn't want to be found?' Rhidian said, and looked pensive.

'Well, he's damn well going to be found,' Rebus exploded. 'We haven't travelled this far to be disappointed.'

'Calm down, Rebus. When we find him we can go from there,' Caleb said sensibly, and eyed the old wizard with a look of indifference. 'We have to find him first.'

'Come on, Red, let's get some supplies together. They must have bags here where we can each carry stuff,' the engineer said, and he and the boy set off below. After a short while everyone was kitted out with a shoulder bag, food and a drink for the journey.

'You can lead us,' Rhidian said as he pointed to the three wizards. Red said nothing and trailed along behind them.

'Everyone, stay together. We don't want to get lost in this place,' Caleb acknowledged everyone with a nod.

It was dawn when they left the stranded ship and Rebus spearheaded the party. All five moved off through the trees in silence.

'You all right to travel?' Caleb asked Alba, concerned that the old man hadn't quite got his strength back since his ordeal.

'Yes, it's fine. Be nice to stretch my legs after all that time cooped up in that cage,' Alba admitted and shrugged his shoulders – the memory brought the disgust he still felt.

The air was humid as the great sun lifted slowly into the sky. The temperature soared as the early morning dew quickly settled into a mist. The heat inside the forest held and their clothes clung to their bodies. It was hard work just to negotiate the deep foliage.

'Keep yourselves hydrated, drink plenty of water,' Rhidian half whispered.

'Why are you talking so quietly, Rhidian?' Red chirped up.

'I don't know, but I've a feeling there maybe more here than we know,' he said. The forest held many sounds of creatures, birds and some grunting sounds that the group didn't want to encounter. They got to a point where the ground dipped and they found themselves by a fallen tree.

The trunk linked two sides of a rather wide ravine. The old tree was rotten and flimsy in places but, unfortunately, the only way to cross. The stream below wasn't deep but the drop to it was – at least ten metres.

'We'll have to go over in single file,' Rebus instructed, and looked further downstream. 'There's doesn't seem to be any other way.'

'I'll go first,' Caleb piped up. 'I can help you from the other side.' He stepped out onto the limb and with the agility of a monkey was soon over there.

'You next, Alba,' Caleb called out. The wizard gingerly made his way across, splaying his arms to balance. Next was Rebus and he took a more speedy approach and didn't falter. Red was up next and he looked really nervous.

'Go on, Red, you can do it. Just take your time,' Rhidian whispered in his ear. Red took a lot longer than the others and gently edged his way over. The log creaked below his feet and seemed to be laughing at him. He was sweating and he almost overbalanced midway – everyone gasped! but he made it.

'Okay, Rhidian, your turn,' Caleb urged. He was last to go. Unbeknown to the others, Rhidian was terrified – more so than Red. He'd fallen down the side of a cliff when he was a kid and that had stayed with him through his entire life. Rebus noticed that there was something troubling him.

'You'll be fine, Rhidian,' Rebus called out in encouragement. 'Don't look down.' These were the words that Rhidian didn't want to hear. Caleb gave Rebus a sharp look of distaste.

'No one wants to hear that,' Caleb whispered to Rebus.

'Come on, Rhidian,' Red shouted, and that unsettled the engineer even more as he stepped on a particularly rotten part of the tree. It gave way and Rhidian fell straight down. He landed with a thud on a small ledge that was jutting out, about a third of the way down. The impact knocked the wind out of his lungs and he lay there not moving.

'I've got a rope,' Caleb said, unwinding it from his shoulder. He tied one end to a tree that was close to the edge and tossed it to where Rhidian had landed. He lowered himself down until he was by his side. Rhidian was coming round and sat up.

'Rhidian, let me tie this around your waist. This ledge isn't going to last long with both our weight on it.' Caleb grimaced. 'Pull him up quickly.' The others pulled and with the combined strength of the three, he was soon hoisted up to safety. 'Quickly it's crumbling,' but even as he said it – it gave way. Caleb braced himself for the long fall, but didn't move an inch once the ledge collapsed. Instead, he was held fast by the combined magic of Rebus and Alba. He floated upwards in a bubble of air and was placed gently at the top.

'Thank you, guys,' Caleb said in gratitude.

'Me too, thanks all. I thought I was a goner,' Rhidian said, still shaken from his near-death experience.

'Let's get out of here before anything else happens,' Rebus insisted.

Damp mist thickened ahead of them and the humidity got unbearable as they moved further along. They were soon at the edge of the forest and it was cooler here, but the mist still danced and swirled before their eyes.

'Where are we?' Rhidian said. He squinted to get some idea, but with the grey barrier blocking everything in sight it was impossible.

'Give it another half an hour and this fog will soon clear,' Rebus commented, the sweat running down his face and chest.

'Yes, that will soon burn away but then we'll be exposed to the sun directly once we're out of this forest,' Alba said, and wiped his forehead with the back of his hand.

'Do not trespass beyond this point,' Red said as he looked at a signpost.

'What's that, boy?' Rebus questioned.

'Look over here. I think it's some kind of burial ground,' the boy explained.

'I get it now,' Rebus realised.

'Get what?' Caleb asked and stood at the sign with the others.

'We've definitely landed in Gelbar. And I don't think we're far away from Obsidian,' Rebus said, his eyes wide with delight.

'What do you mean?' Caleb quizzed.

'How are you so certain?' Rhidian posed the question.

'Gold,' Alba spoke up.

'Yes, gold,' Rebus smiled. 'This is the burial ground of the unfortunate. These are the miners who dug for gold and lost their lives in the attempt. This is their final resting place and no one should disturb or trespass the ground. But there's no other way around and it's too dense to go looking. We have to cut through the graveyard. Everyone with me?' There were nervous nods from the rest.

Reluctantly they walked beyond the trespass sign – each kept their eyes sharp and as they walked through the spiritual peace, fear filled each and every one.

Chapter 21
The Mine

The five figures felt almost invisible as they ambled amongst the dead. No one spoke for a time until the dense heat of the day soon turned cold. The clothes they wore were damp and uncomfortable in the heat – now clung to their bodies like heavy armour. Red shivered and he found it hard to breathe. Something was happening and he was scared to think what it might be. He darted his gaze in every direction and craned his neck from side-to-side. His stomach was so tight he felt as though he wanted to be sick.

'I don't like this,' he said in little than a whisper, and imagined the gravestones rising up. 'We shouldn't be here,' he complained. 'It's not right.'

'Red, stay close – we'll be fine,' Rhidian assured him, and his soft voice seemed to calm the youngster, but not for long. The grey curtain that engulfed them was slowly giving up its secrets. Headstones and crosses appeared with scary-looking wrought iron statues. The graveyard had been long forgotten and the decay was all too obvious. No one came here to honour these dead – death showed itself in every designed sculpture and weeping cherub. 'I don't like it here,' Red repeated and shivered in cold.

'Take it easy, boy. We won't be here long,' Rebus,' said through the gloom. 'We'll find a way out further up I expect, and we'll soon be back in the sun. Now get a grip.'

'Stick with us and don't wander off,' Caleb uttered in a hushed tone.

'As if I'm going to wander off in here,' Red retorted with a tremble in his voice.

'This doesn't feel right,' Rhidian added to the conversation. 'I'm inclined to agree with Red.'

'I know what you mean,' Alba gushed. 'The dead should be left to sleep.'

'What was that?' Red was flinching at every shadow. His mouth was dry and he anxiously took a gulp from the bottle he carried in his bag.

'It's nothing, Red, you're just jumpy,' Caleb said, and reached out and touched his shoulder for comfort. Red gave a jerk. 'Wow, Red, it's only me, take it easy.' Caleb snatched back his hand and held it up in surrender.

'S-sorry Caleb,' he stammered. 'I-I'm scared,' he whispered, and didn't mind telling Caleb, who he knew wouldn't mock him.

'It's all right, Red. I totally understand. Stick by me,' Caleb advised and smiled. Red trembled; the damp clothes made his skin prickle. He took a few short breaths and walked closer to the wizard. They continued on, but picked up the pace. They were all in a hurry to get out of there.

There was clear sound and everyone heard it. It was a clinking noise, like wine glasses being toasted but not quite so sharp.

'What's that?' Rhidian spoke through the mist.

'Everyone stop,' Rebus commanded. All five stood, each one breathing heavily. The grey swirls weaved between the plots – images sharpened and faded as the scene played with their eyes.

'If I didn't know any better, I would say this place is alive not dead!' Rhidian gasped. Another weird sound caught their attention.

'Anyone hear that?' Rebus hissed. No one answered – they just strained their ears; eyes peered into the fog. There it was again, but this time there was a dull thudding sound added to it, like bamboo wind chimes clicking in the breeze. Rebus said something under his breath. Soon all five of them realised they were holding *swords*! They'd just appeared in their hands.

'What is going on?' Rhidian rasped and peered at the blade he was now carrying. It had a long, slim blade and a ribbed handle, which made it easy to grip. Again, no one answered. Soon, darkened figures grinned through the grainy façade and made themselves known.

'It's the dead,' Rebus called out. 'They've come back! Defend yourselves,' he cried, booming through the quiet. Red had never held a sword before, never mind used one. Neither had Rhidian. He was holding his awkwardly as if it was a wrench.

The mist began to peel away and, in its place, revealed what could only be described as an army of the deceased. There were hundreds of figures of all shapes, mostly male, still dressed in their mining clothes. Long lost souls, maybe killed doing their jobs and dragged out here and buried!

For the first few seconds there was a standoff. These skeletal beings, stood silent. The small band of travellers were surrounded and the only way through was to fight. Caleb let out a battle roar.

'ATTACK!' he bellowed, moved forward with purpose and slashed at the enemy, and took two of the skeletons' heads clean off; their bodies collapsed to the ground in a pile of bones.

Red felt a cold, bony grip around his throat and froze. He was face-to-face with a skull – empty eye sockets and a toothless jaw. The creature gripped with both skeletal hands and squeezed. Red was taken completely by surprise and began to choke and gasped for breath. The stench of rotten bones filled his nostrils and his eyes bulged from their sockets. He was feeling sleepy and dropped his sword. His body felt light, as if he could float away and nothing else mattered. Suddenly, there was a sharp snap and the strangling grip released and fell away. Red fell to the ground, coughing and gulping for breath.

'Red fight back!' Caleb bellowed. 'Don't just sit there or they will kill you,' Caleb raged. When Red came to, he could hear the sounds of battle. He saw the others – they were all fighting for their lives, and charging their way through the swarm of skeletons. Another zombie miner approached and when the boy looked up it seemed to be grinning at him. It had the remains of a cloth garment hanging from its shoulder to its waist and it was carrying a dagger.

Red suddenly felt that if he didn't fight back his life would be over. Without thinking, he picked up his sword and sliced at the attacker. It was like fighting a hat stand. As soon as his sword impacted, the skeleton crumpled into a pile of bones… but there were more and he had to help the others keep the hordes away. He began slashing like a demented windmill. The dead attacked from everywhere, but Red, Rhidian and the rest had the upper hand. They were alive!

'I can see a building ahead,' Rebus cried. 'Let's make for that. Maybe we can hold them off in there.'

The mist had almost lifted completely and the morbid reality showed itself. There were hundreds of dead souls rising from the graves, far too many for them to defend against. The small band of travellers looked on in utter disbelief.

'Follow Rebus!' Caleb shouted. 'Don't let him out of your sight.'

The five of them moved faster and forced their way forward, chopping and crunching bones. The more they appeared to *kill*, the more appeared in their place. It was hopeless.

The building ahead was a huge monument built into the mountain. Its entrance was boarded with old timbers.

'There's no other way around. We'll have to get inside and block the entrance!' Rhidian shouted breathlessly. The only problem now was the fact that some of the zombie horde had realised where the wizards and mortals were headed.

'We're almost there. Come on, fight,' Caleb ranted. He was right; only a few more metres and they would be at the entrance.

'Break through the timber!' Rebus screamed, as he fought off two attackers at the same time. Rhidian and Red used their swords to smash open the barricade. The rotten wood gave in easily and left a cloud of brown dust in its wake.

'Come on, we're in!' Rhidian screamed. The engineer and the boy slipped inside first and the wizards backed their way in behind them.

'What's happening to them?' Alba said, and looked really confused.

'They've stopped attacking,' Caleb realised. He was right; every single soul in the graveyard had ceased their fight and were slowly returning back to whence they came. The mist had mysteriously reappeared and each body turned and slowly walked back into the grey depths, until they'd all dissolved into the ground. The five friends stood at the opening and looked on in breathless bewilderment.

'What just happened?' Red questioned.

'They won't enter here for some reason,' Rebus surmised.

'If they fear entering here, then what do you think awaits us inside?' Caleb asked.

'I-I'm not sure I want to go any further,' Red admitted.

'Red, please think about this for one moment. You can either come along with us, and we'll go in there together. We'll look after you, you know that,' the engineer said, as he pointed into the gloom that awaited them. 'Or, you can go back out there… and you know what is waiting for us there, don't you? For me, there really isn't a choice. We've only just about made it in here.' Red didn't answer and only nodded. Rhidian grinned back at him and ruffled his shaggy hair. He smiled and sucked in a mouthful of air. 'We are ready? Rhidian grinned at Red and nodded to Rebus.

'Okay. We all set? Then off we go,' Rebus said with conviction.

Now, with the battle over, the swords disappeared and they were all left in darkness. None of them knew if it was a better bet going forward, but it was much better than going back into the graveyard. So, they reluctantly moved further in.

Chapter 22
Deep underground

The light from outside was soon swallowed up by the dense darkness from within.

'Don't move, anyone.' Rebus' voice cut through the pitched black. There was a flicker of white and then a blue flame appeared out of nowhere. The fire was dancing in the palm of Rebus' hand. Red looked on in awe, his eyes squinting at the brightness.

'Doesn't that hurt?' he asked, and winced at the thought.

'Not for a wizard,' Rebus replied, pleased with the fact that his magic came quite easily now. 'This is the norm.' There was a grin on his face, the smugness of someone who knew he'd impressed the boy.

'There's a lantern hanging just there.' Alba indicated to a small oil lamp that hung on a nail. Rebus tentatively walked over to it and lifted it off the bracket. He shook it vigorously and was happy to hear the slopping of liquid inside. He raised the glass dome and blew light from his hand onto the wick – it lit instantly. A vibrant flame soon flowered inside the glass and the immediate area was suddenly bathed in yellow.

'Hey, look.' Red sounded excited. The boy wasn't standing, but kneeling on the ground. There was a pile of timber on the ground too. He'd pulled all the loose boards to one side. Once he'd done that, he realised that they'd concealed the beginning of a tram track. He peered back through the gloom and could see that the roadway was buried. The years of neglect and falling dust had covered the iron. Red got up and stepped over the remaining jagged boards. He stood at the mouth of the mine.

'Well done, lad,' Rhidian said. 'I think Red has revealed our path.'

'Well, my instincts tell me that what we're looking for may be in there somewhere.' Rebus stabbed at the darkness.

'I've also got the same feeling,' Caleb spoke with certainty.

'Me, too,' Alba added.

'Red, are you ready to go?' Rhidian asked, and put his hand on the boy's shoulder and gave it a gentle squeeze.

'Not really, but I know there's no other way,' he relented.

Rebus lifted the lamp and began the journey along the tracks. The rest followed in single file. The track dropped down into the belly of the mineshaft. Everyone kept pace with Rebus – none wanted to be left scurrying in the dark.

'Hold on, Rebus,' Caleb called out, and the group stopped. 'Give me a hand with this, boys,' he said, and moved over to one side of the tunnel.

'What have you found?' Red rasped from the shadows, his voice dry.

'Look, a tram,' Caleb said, and sounded happy. The tram was on its side and obviously hadn't been used in years. It was covered in dust and spiders.

'That's what they used to get the gold out,' Rebus informed them.

'Yeah, well now it can transport us into the mine instead of us walking. It's got a brake that still seems to work by the look of it.' Caleb's voice echoed as he inspected the vehicle and wrenched the handle backwards and forwards. So Caleb, Red, Rhidian and Rebus groaned, heaved and wrestled, until it flipped over onto its wheels. Alba wanted to help, but Red wouldn't let him. He was still too weak and so held the lamp. They managed to fix it into place on the rail track. There was an upright bar on the front with a hook and Alba placed the lamp on it. But when they tried to get the car moving, it wouldn't budge.

'The wheels are seized up,' Caleb complained. 'All that work for nothing.'

'Hold on,' Rhidian said, and disappeared for a moment. When he came back, he was carrying a small oil can. He had a huge grin on his face.

'Where did you get… oh, I forgot we have an engineer in our midst,' Caleb joked. Rhidian ignored him and set about oiling the wheels. He pumped the trigger and the oil spurted through the nozzle. He greased all four until they were spinning freely.

'I assumed that where there's a tram, there had to be something close by to repair and oil it. We'll have to give it a bit of a push to get the thing working,' Rhidian explained.

'Okay, what if we get in and one of us push? I mean, that way the weight in the tram should force the wheels to move,' Alba said sensibly.

'Sounds like a good idea, Alba,' Rebus praised.

'Who wants to push?' Rebus asked, and looked at the others. He didn't really add himself to the equation.

'I'll do it,' Red said.

'Well done, lad,' Rebus gushed.

'Yeah, well you old gits would be out of puff and wouldn't be able to climb back in,' he said with a chuckle.

'You cheeky young scamp,' Rebus scolded, but smiled.

'No, I'll do it,' Rhidian piped up. 'No offence, Red, but we need a bit of weight behind it.' Red looked miffed and reluctantly jumped into the car.

'Hah,' Rebus chuckled.

'Right, now that's settled, let's all get in.' Rebus was in no mood to hang around any longer. The four of them climbed in and that left just enough room for one more, and a little bit spare for elbowroom. But, even with the combined weight of the four people, the tram still didn't move.

'Right, hold on in there and try and put all your weight to the front,' Rhidian instructed. He leaned his right shoulder into the tram and pushed as hard as he could. The engineer grunted and groaned but nothing moved. 'Put some more oil on the wheels,' he asked with a grunt. So, Caleb poured more oil onto the axle.

'Try again,' Caleb prompted. Once again, Rhidian put all his weight behind the metal carriage and, with more grunting, there was suddenly a crack that echoed down the mine.

'It's beginning to move!' Rebus shouted. Everyone leaned over the front and, with the weight transference, it started to move.

'Red, jump out and push with me,' Rhidian insisted. Red leapt out of the car and joined him at the back. The vehicle juddered and slowly screeched as if in agony; all the while Caleb was applying the oil. The car edged forward until it began to gain momentum and then, whoosh, it was free. Rhidian and Red fell over onto the track.

'Apply the brake, for God's sake!' Rhidian screamed from the ground. Caleb dropped the oil can and dived for the lever. He pulled back and the car slowed down and eventually stopped.

'Come on, you two,' Rebus complained. 'We haven't got all day.' Rhidian looked hard at Rebus as he got to his feet. Red followed him to the waiting car. The engineer positioned himself next to the brake and Caleb let him take over. The others slotted into their places.

'Let's go,' Rhidian uttered, and released the brake. The tram began rolling down the track again.

'Keep it steady!' Rebus shouted over the sound of the click-click-click of the wheels. 'If there's any debris on the track, which is very likely, then we can stop in time.'

'Will do,' Rhidian responded.

It was mostly dark as they swished through the tunnel. The only source of light was the lantern, which didn't make a lot of difference in the grand scheme of things. Red closed his eyes and let the rush of the wind caress his face. It felt kind of exciting to him as the tram picked up speed. Rebus stood peering as far into the darkness as he could.

'Everyone, keep your eyes peeled!' he shouted, as the rush of air whooshed past his ears.

Soon the tram was running freely – the oil by now had worked its way into the axle. The rails seemed in good repair. Rhidian relaxed on the brake, but kept his wits about him in case he had to stop abruptly. Soon the channel they travelled along opened out into a wide cavern. The lamp's rays dimmed in the humongous expanse.

'Slow it down, Rhidian.' Rebus sounded agitated.

'What's the problem?' Rhidian shouted, as he tried to lift his voice above the noise of the wheels and rushing air.

'I think I see a bridge ahead,' Rebus shouted, his tone echoed. He was right; soon everyone could hear the hollow sound of the track beneath. They could only assume how high up they were, as the depth was just a mass of black tar. They could feel the tram pick up speed.

'We're going too fast. Slow us down!' Rebus bellowed. Rhidian did as asked and pulled hard on the brake. Clouds of blue smoke rose from the wooden block which ground against the metal rim of the wheel. The car wasn't slowing fast enough.

'Slow us down, Rhidian. There's...' Rebus' voice trailed off.

'What's the matter?' Caleb peered over Alba's shoulder and his mouth dropped open. He quickly turned to Rhidian.

'There's a break in the track, there's a break in the track,' he repeated, his face contorted, eyes wide. He quickly gripped the lever with Rhidian and pulled.

'No, Caleb, don't!' Rhidian pleaded, but it was too late. The wooden handle broke off under the heavy pressure – now the tram ran free. Caleb fell backwards and landed on top of Red.

'Stop, stop it now!' Rebus screamed. But it was even too late to use his magic to help them. The gap in the track was on them before anyone could really react.

'Hold on everyone!' Caleb screeched. The carriage zoomed off the rails – it sailed through the blackness for a moment or so in slow motion, or so it appeared. The timbers had collapsed into the depths, leaving a four-metre gap. There was nothing they could do, only hold on and wait for the inevitable. The excessive speed carried the tram through the space in between. It came crashing down the other side, almost landing directly on the waiting track but not quite. It impacted, twisted, flipped over and threw everyone out. The sound of crashing metal and the smell of scorched wood filled the air. And then silence... the darkness engulfed the lamp when it smashed and the flame diminished...

Chapter 23
A Split Decision

The air was dense with the dust from the crash. Rhidian came to and could barely breathe. He began to cough and he tried to clear his throat. He pushed himself into a sitting position and found that everything ached. But he suspected that he hadn't broken any bones. He coughed some more and peered into the tunnel. It took him a couple of seconds to realise that he wasn't in complete darkness any longer. He could actually see his companions and, as it happened, the state of the tram. It was completely smashed beyond repair.

'Aw,' he groaned, deep in the pit of his stomach. He shook it off as if it were insignificant. They'd have to walk now, that was all.

'Is everyone all right?' he rasped; his voice was hoarse as he struggled to create spit inside his mouth. He could hear movement from the others. Surprisingly, they were left in twilight. There was a haze that shone through the dust. The five of them got to their feet and rubbed off the excess dirt from the mine.

'Where's that light coming from?' Caleb asked sharply, and shielded his eyes. He realised he could see the others. He looked up and there was a small fissure in the roof of the cave, which let in much needed light. The rail stretched on through to the depths of the mine. The cloud of dust eventually settled like baking powder on a cake.

'No broken bones?' Rebus said as he looked around. 'Well that's lucky.'

'You okay, Alba?' Red's voice seared through from the shadow.

'Yep, I'm fine, young man,' Alba reported.

'What about you, Red? Are you hurt?' he asked.

'Nope, I'm all right too. Bit sore, I suppose, but okay,' he answered.

'Is that tram still in working order, do you think?' Caleb stood and peered at the upturned cart.

'I'm afraid not.' Rhidian stooped down to examine it more closely. 'The wheels are buckled and one has come off completely,' he said. 'The wood frame is shot, too,' he said.

'Well, we're on foot from here on in,' Caleb expressed, not relishing the walk ahead.

'Aw, that was fun,' Red chuckled. Rebus rolled his eyes.

'Anyone want a drink? I've some water here,' Rhidian offered, after he'd found his shoulder bag.

'I think we're fine,' Red said as he looked at the others.

'Is the lamp working?' Alba added sensibly.

'Nah, that's gone too,' Caleb said, when he found the broken glass and a pool of oil.

'We'll have to follow the track, I suppose.' Rebus looked into the distance, scratching his head. 'We were making up so much ground too. Dammit!' He grimaced through gritted teeth.

'It couldn't be helped, old man,' Rhidian said.

'I know,' Rebus relented, a little perplexed, but was soon upbeat again. He smiled when he discovered another lamp on a post next to him. Probing further, he could see a metal container next to it. Rebus flipped open the old tobacco tin and, to his delight, found dry matches. 'The miners who originally worked the mine must have kept lamps hanging in various places throughout the mine,' he mumbled. So, he grabbed the metal box and put it in his rucksack. He also unhooked the oil lamp and let is hang by his side.

'Come on then, we've a wizard to find,' Red piped up positively. He then started to make his way down the slope. The others followed without a word. Rhidian grinned to himself; the boy was becoming more responsible.

No one spoke for a while as the small band of men descended into the depths of the mine. The light paled as the passageway narrowed and it was back to darkness again. Rebus diligently lit the lamp and stepped up to the front to lead again. The sound of heavy footprints and panting breath filled the cavern, only to be added by the drip-drip-drip of water streaming down the walls.

'Everything looks the same,' Rebus grumbled as he pushed through the gloomy veil. He had to stop suddenly and was almost trampled by the others.

'What's going on?' Rhidian spoke from the back.

'Yeah, why've we stopped?' Red piped up.

'There's a fork,' Rebus spoke up.

'Great, I'm starving. What's for dinner?' Red said cheerfully.

'Not that kind of fork, stupid boy,' Rebus muttered. Alba and the rest giggled in the background. Rebus turned and everyone stopped like scolded school children.

'Which way do we take?' Alba enquired. Both ways looked very similar.

'Rebus, give me the lamp,' Caleb gestured with his hands. 'I'll walk down the left one and see if there's any clues as to where it leads.'

Rebus reluctantly handed him the light. He disappeared into the left side and was gone for a couple of minutes. His footsteps faded as quickly as the glowing lamp. He soon reappeared and said nothing. He then made his way down the right corridor, leaving the others in darkness once again.

In roughly about the same amount of time, he returned with a blank look on his face and handed the lamp back to Rebus.

'There doesn't seem to be much difference in the two,' Caleb said.

'What do we do then?' Red hissed impatiently. 'We can't just hang around here.'

'I say we try the two,' Alba said after much quietness.

'What? Split up?' Rhidian confirmed.

'Well that way we get to cover the two directions. Maybe if one finds the right one, they can go back and get the other team,' Alba reasoned.

'Hold on, what about the lamp? We only have one,' Rebus reminded them. 'One team can't go around stumbling in the dark.'

'Not true,' Caleb retorted with a look of smugness, and he lifted his left hand, revealing another lamp.

'Fantastic. Where did you get that?' Rebus said with a look of shock.

'I just saw it on the ground, inside the left tunnel,' he revealed.

'Who is going with who then?' Red cut in.

'Who is going with whom?' Rebus corrected, and Red countered with a wrinkle of his nose.

'Whatever,' he grunted. Rhidian knew they hadn't clicked as friends from the beginning, so did Caleb.

'What if I take Red with me down this one?' Caleb said, and pointed to the left fork. He wanted to keep the peace between the two. 'And *you*, Rhidian and Alba can take that one?' Caleb concluded, and hoped Rebus would agree.

'Sounds good to me,' Red chipped in quickly, frowning at Rebus in the process.

'Yes, all right, we'll do it that way.' Rebus was as happy to rid himself of the boy as Red was eager to rid himself of Rebus.

Caleb lit his lamp from the flame of the other and they were ready to depart.

'Let's do this!' Red shrieked with excitement.

'Don't seem so eager, young man. You don't know what's down there,' Rebus added smartly and added, 'take care, the both of you.' Caleb nudged Red in the back, and when he looked at Caleb, nodded to reciprocate.

'Yeah,' the boy replied, 'you take care, too.' He looked at Rhidian, Alba and, finally, Rebus. There was a respectful nod from both sides and Red turned away.

'If any of us find something, we'll meet back at this point,' Caleb instructed. There was a general understanding of the agreement from both parties and, with that, they all set off on their separate ways. Soon they couldn't hear each other any more, and the quest to find Obsidian continued.

Chapter 24
Underground River

Caleb lifted the lamp up high, just as Rebus had been doing. The tunnel was as damp and dismal as the one they'd left behind. The uneven walls glistened yellow from the glow of the flame. The ground was tricky to walk on, with rocks and diverts obstructing the way. As they moved along, all they could hear were their grinding, echoed footsteps and the sound of water everywhere.

'Yuk,' Red exclaimed.

'What's the matter?' Caleb asked.

'Some water dripped down my neck,' Red said with a shiver. Caleb laughed.

'Tell me, what is it with you and Rebus, anyway?' Caleb questioned.

'That old guy always rubs me up the wrong way. I can't do anything right when he's around,' Red complained.

'Old guy. Now I know why you're always banging heads,' Caleb grinned. 'No one likes being called old.' Red looked nonplussed as he followed behind.

'What happens when we find Obsidian?' Red asked.

'Now, that's going to be one of the toughest questions to answer. I don't know Obsidian, but he may not want to go back to Valusha,' Caleb admitted.

'But it's his home,' Red reminded him, and stumbled over a particularly awkward patch of ground.

'I know that and so do you, but with Jenta-Lor to confront, maybe he won't relish the challenge,' Caleb responded. 'Perhaps he's even happy where he is.'

'Wow, didn't even think of that. You may be right. But all I want to do is get my life back to normal on Valusha,' Red said with a puff. 'I certainly don't want to go back to that prison.'

'Red, you won't, don't worry about that,' Caleb assured him. Caleb didn't speak much after that and continued on in silence through the mountain. The ground fell into a long declining corridor. The walls were closing in on them, too.

'Why would anyone want to live down here?' Red grimaced. It was getting so tight; he had to twist his body in order to get through the gap.

'This is probably the reason someone *is* living down here, Red... did you think of that?' Caleb retorted.

'What do you mean?' the boy said, as they finally slid through to a bigger space.

'Well, if it deterred people from coming down here, then if Obsidian *is* in hiding he wouldn't have to worry too much about someone finding him, would he?' Caleb said sensibly. Red didn't answer; he just looked thoughtful and nodded in compliance. Just then, Caleb stopped walking. He could feel a strange sensation in his stomach. There was something wrong. Red stopped too when he saw Caleb standing there.

'What's the matter, Caleb? What's wrong?' Red asked; there was concern in his voice and a knot tightened in the pit of his belly.

'Shhh.' Caleb put his finger to his lips. 'I don't know,' he said. 'But it's not good – get down,' he added urgently. Red immediately did as he was asked and the two of them crouched on the ground beneath a large rock.

Caleb edged up to the top of the boulder so that he could see more clearly. They were in an open cave on a small ledge. Not even the lamp could penetrate the full darkness in here. They could hear loose rocks roll freely down the cliff face. The old wizard lifted the lamp, but not too high so that they'd get noticed in their hiding place. He peered down to the ground. There was an open expanse and, beyond that, nothing. Caleb scratched at his cheek.

'What's happening?' Red hissed.

'It's a dead end,' Caleb answered, and sounded downbeat. It was as if he were searching for a solution. He looked again at the wall of rock opposite. It looked solid enough from what he could make out. Red sensed that Caleb was tense; he didn't know how, but he could feel his companion's turmoil.

'There's something going on, isn't there?' Red spoke more calmly, not more than a whisper. Caleb said nothing, but had spotted something – a ripple of heat, maybe. *Heat*, down here? No, it was… it was definitely… ah, a trickle of magic! He looked again, now sure on where it emanated – there it was again. It could be a spell cast down there, or some kind of illusion – he was certain of it now.

'What have you found?' Red was so close that Caleb could feel his breath against his cheek.

'It'll be a trap to stop mortals getting through. Or even strong enough to stop wizards, too,' Caleb guessed.

'What do we do, Caleb?' Red asked. 'We can't go back.'

'We'll have to go down there first, and then face it head on,' Caleb said, his tone casual.

'But it's only an illusion, right?' It can't hurt us… can it?' Red sounded scared – after all, he was mortal.

'All magic is dangerous, Red – even a mask of magic,' Caleb said knowingly. 'We just have to counter it and break through. The tricky part is getting down there.' He pointed to the perilous slope before them. 'I'm also going to have to put out the lamp!'

'B-but how are we going to see where we're going?' Red stammered.

'I'll relight it at the bottom. I can't risk whatever that is, seeing us coming,' Caleb admitted. Red swallowed hard. 'Are we ready?' Caleb asked, as a smile lifted his old features.

'Why are you smiling?' Red questioned.

'I'd rather die with a smile on my face,' he said cheerily. Red looked at him and arched his eyebrow in confusion. But he didn't have time to say any more. Caleb dowsed the flame and disappeared over the top. Red had no choice but to quickly follow.

The first part wasn't too bad and felt quite solid. They had to navigate their way down by sitting on their backsides, using their heels as a kind of brake. Red couldn't see Caleb and assumed he was just ahead of him. He also had to use his hands, palm-down to steady his descent.

The ground soon became tricky as the loose shale broke the tension of the surface. Once that happened, there was no amount of heel braking that could stop Red from sliding. He lost complete control and found himself torpedoing down the cliff face. Rocks tumbled from all angles and the boy, not wanting to, twisted sideways, eventually ending upside-down.

'Ca-leb, I'm fal-ling,' he rattled, as he picked up momentum and tumbled uncontrollably down the mountainside. It was dark as soot and his head was spinning so much that he didn't know what was happening. All he could hear was the echoed cracking of rocks and the heavy flow of shale. He felt small stones bang against his body and one cracked the side of his skull. He was lightheaded and felt sick... and finally blacked out.

*****

'Are you okay?' Rhidian asked.

'I'm fine, honestly,' Alba assured him. 'In fact, I'm feeling a lot stronger now that I've eaten and had some exercise.' Rebus turned and looked at his friend, the light from the lantern illuminating their faces.

'That's good,' Rebus added. 'You were cramped up in that filthy cage for a while. I'll make sure that never happens again.' He seemed resolute.

The air smelled stale and damp for a while, but they soon tasted fresh and pure air.

'Where is that coming from?' Rhidian had noticed the difference right away.

'There's got to be a fissure above us somewhere letting in clean air, I imagine.' Alba greedily sucked in the clean oxygen. It felt good after the stale air they'd been used too. Soon after, they all heard the gush of water. It got a lot louder as they approached a small underground river.

'Hold up,' Rebus said urgently.

'What's the matter?' Rhidian chirped up.

'We've a problem!' Rebus announced.

'Oh, my,' Alba said, when he and Rhidian stepped shoulder-to-shoulder. It *was* a major problem. The river cut through the rocks and was flowing at a rate of knots. It was about four metres wide and looked impossible to cross.

'What are we going to do?' Alba squeaked.

'We have to go back,' Rhidian said.

'That'll add God knows how much time to our journey,' Rebus rasped.

'We could meet up with the others in the other tunnel and get past this that way,' Alba added.

'Who's to say that they're not already following us? Their tunnel could be a dead-end too, and we'd be right back where we started,' Rebus continued, but sounded angry.

'We're going to vote on it,' Rhidian said adamantly.

'We're not. We have to...' Rebus stopped talking.

'What's that?' Alba strained his ears and tried to make out a background noise. The rush of the river was so loud that it was hard to hear anything.

'It sounds like a rock fall!' Rhidian shouted.

'Is that – the boy?' Rebus' voice echoed.

'Yes, Red and Caleb are in trouble,' Rhidian bellowed. 'We have to help them. They're ahead of us.'

'How? We can't get past this river,' Alba reminded them.

'We haven't got a rope, or anything to bridge the gap.' Rhidian stood helpless.

'But we do have two wizards,' Alba cut in.

'Magic?' Rhidian said and looked at Rebus and Alba.

'It's going to take everything we have,' Rebus added, and peered at Alba. 'You up to it, old man?'

'There's only one way to find out.' Alba actually looked as though he was going to enjoy the experience.

'A transfer, I think,' Rebus announced and Alba nodded. Rhidian looked at the two of them, bewilderment in his eyes.

'Come sit, Rhidian. We must all hold hands.' Rebus outstretched his hand in a gesture for him to join them.

'Wh-at? I'm involved too? Cool,' Rhidian grinned.

'Yep,' Alba chirped.

'So, what do I do?' The engineer was suddenly filled with a childish excitement.

'Actually, nothing! You just have to hold on,' Alba said.

They sat crossed-legged with the lamp in the centre. The next thing to happen was for them to hold hands. Rhidian couldn't believe what he was doing and felt like a little kid in the playground in kindergarten.

'Close your eyes, Rhidian. We haven't much time,' Rebus said. He did as asked and held onto the two wizards. He closed his eyes, but still felt silly. He sat for a moment and then couldn't keep quiet any longer.

'What now, Rebus?' he asked, but realised that he wasn't holding anyone's hand any more.

'Rhidian, help me.' Rhidian heard Alba's voice next to him. He opened his eyes and could see the lamp still in front of him, but he wasn't on the same patch of ground. In fact, the two sorcerers weren't there, either. Alba was outstretched along the cave floor and Rhidian could see why. Rebus was in the water, being pulled along by the current of the river. The engineer quickly gripped his left arm; Alba already had hold of his right.

'Pull him in!' Alba shouted, but his voice was laboured. 'I'm losing my grip,' he strained. Rhidian only had the sleeve of Rebus' shirt. The river's power was too much and Alba had to let go.

Rhidian kept hold of the material of Rebus' cuff and tried to grip his shoulder with his right hand. There was the sound of ripping material and the next thing... Rebus was gone! Rhidian was left holding his sleeve.

'No, no!' Rhidian screamed.

'It's no use, my boy. He's gone!' Alba said; the look of utter loss engulfed his whole face.

'We've got to find him. He could still be alive,' Rhidian insisted.

'We have to help Red and Caleb now, Rhidian. They're in danger too,' Alba insisted. 'We can't do any more for Rebus.' That last sentence felt so final to Rhidian that his stomach twisted and a heavy sadness consumed him. He wiped his eyes and mopped the snot from his nose. Alba patted him on the shoulder and picked up the lamp. 'We have to go, Rhidian,' Alba said solemnly. Rhidian nodded and didn't say anything. He hadn't known Rebus for long but felt as though they had hit it off from the start. He placed Rebus' sleeve on the bank and walked away with his head bowed.

Chapter 25
Rescue

Rhidian pushed on for a short while and eventually felt he had to speak up.

'Alba, how can you seem so hard?' he asked.

'Now is not the time, Rhidian. We have to help Red and Caleb. I'll talk of this later.' Rhidian appeared shocked, but didn't ask anything more and Alba led the way as quickly as he could.

They climbed over loose rocks and shale, which obscured the landscape.

'Alba, would you like me to take the lamp?' he asked, when he saw the old wizard struggling to climb and hold on to the lantern.

'If you wouldn't mind, Rhidian,' Alba replied. When he turned to the engineer, Rhidian could plainly see tears in his eyes and realised at that point Alba was indeed missing his friend dearly.

'I'm sorry,' Rhidian responded, and Alba gave a respective nod. They clambered over debris until the light from the lamp revealed a silhouette. It appeared to be hunched on the ground.

'Hey there. Who are you?' Alba called out.

'Alba, is that you?' The answer came back. 'It's me – Caleb,' the wizard responded. Rhidian and Alba rushed over to him as quickly as they could, but it was difficult. The stones moved and dirt and rocks trickled down the slope.

They soon discovered that Caleb was kneeling over the body of Red. The boy was still and ridged as a board.

'What happened?' Rhidian's voice echoed, his face filled with concern.

'The stones tumbled down behind us,' Caleb explained. 'I think Red caught a rock to his head,' he said, and pointed to the clotted blood that congealed around the boy's temple.

'It's only a graze, Caleb. He'll be fine. He's just been knocked unconscious. I'm sure he'll come round any minute,' Alba assured him, and dipped in his pocket. He pulled out a small bottle with a cork in the neck. He removed the cork and wafted the bottle under Red's nose. Red began to stir, so Alba replaced the cork and dropped the bottle back into his pocket. Red opened his eyes and tried to speak.

'Don't talk, just take it easy, and take a sip of this.' Rhidian gave him a bottle of water. He immediately sat up, and that made him dizzy. He wobbled and almost slumped to one side.

'Wow, take it easy, Red,' Rhidian said, as he steadied the boy.

'Aw, what happened?' Red mumbled. 'Oh, hold on, I remember... I tumbled down that slope following Caleb.'

'That's right, Red,' Caleb agreed, kneeling over the boy.

'Hey, where did you guys come from? And where's Rebus?' Red pressed.

'Yeah, where's Rebus?' Caleb joined in. He was as surprised as the boy. The look on Rhidian and Alba's face was enough to tell the story. But Alba took it upon himself to explain the whole thing.

'No,' Red said, and looked really upset; his eyes glazed and two streams of tears rolled down his cheeks. 'I can't believe it. I mean, we did knock heads now and again, but that didn't mean that I didn't like or respect him.'

'We know,' Rhidian added. 'It was mostly banter.'

'That's awful.' Caleb was as cut-up as the rest. 'When we've finished all this, we'll have to respect him by planning a wizard's funeral,' Caleb said, sadness in his eyes.

'Yes, we've been beating ourselves up too about why we couldn't save him.' Rhidian still carried the guilt.

'It wasn't our fault. Hell, it wasn't anyone's fault, Rhidian. These things are out of our control,' Alba cursed. 'Now what we've got to do is fill in his wishes and find Obsidian. Then get him to go back to Valusha, where we can pay tribute to him in a proper ceremony.'

'I agree,' Red said, as he wiped away the wetness from his nose.

'Me too,' Caleb also decided.

'I'm in,' Rhidian said.

'That leaves me, and I'm with you,' Alba concluded.

'That's great,' Red added.

'So, what's been happening? Why are you down here?' Rhidian enquired, changing the subject from the sadness.

'There's this rock pile,' Caleb explained. Rhidian looked at the wall of boulders.

'Yeah, and?' he responded.

'That's not right,' Alba interrupted. 'It feels... I don't know, weird. There is magic at play here.'

'Just what I thought,' Caleb agreed.

'What's not right? What's weird?' Rhidian pressed.

'That pile of rocks isn't really there,' Alba clarified.

'But I can see it,' Rhidian insisted and appeared confused.

'No, you're seeing what you're supposed to be seeing,' Caleb said, his eyes narrow in thought. 'That... is a clever disguise that only an experienced wizard would conjure. I'm not saying it is

Obsidian, but whoever set this in place is pretty powerful.' Deep down he suspected it to be Obsidian.

'A smoke screen?' Rhidian asked curiously.

'Yes, a camouflaged *entrance*?' Red piped up, filled with curiosity and excitement. He peered at the granite and licked his lips in anticipation.

'Well done, young man… an entrance indeed,' Alba praised.

'How do we get in?' Rhidian's keenness was spiked also.

'Now that's the question.' There was a pause from the wizard. 'I think we have to… walk through and find out,' Caleb said simply, and smiled as he said it.

'Are you both sure?' Rhidian asked, but didn't look at all convinced. 'Would it just be that simple? There could also be danger on the other side.'

'We're sure,' the wizards said in unison.

'Rhidian, if you didn't know any better, and because you're not a wizard, and we weren't here to inform you, then it would probably appear as solid rock. It would actually feel solid, because your mind would tell you so,' Alba explained.

'I wouldn't have had a second thought. Wow, the wizard thing is a lot more complicated than mechanical stuff,' Rhidian admitted. 'I'll just stick with what I know, and go with the flow.'

'Will you be all right to get up, Red?' Caleb asked in concern.

'Yeah, think I'm okay now,' the boy responded and Caleb reached out his hand and he gripped it. The boy ached a little as he got to his feet, but was otherwise fine.

'Come on then, let's not waste any more time,' Alba said, and took the lamp and held it aloft. He took a deep breath and cleared his mind.

Chapter 26
The Entrance

They stood at the base of the pile of boulders. To Rhidian, it still looked solid, but the others were convinced that it was an illusion.

'Well, what do we do now? That looks pretty solid to me.' Rhidian had second thoughts about the whole business.

'It'll be fine, Rhidian, trust me,' Alba replied. Caleb and Alba looked at one another and Red flicked a gaze to Rhidian, who was shaking his head and raking his fingers through his sandy hair.

Tentatively, all four moved forward into the rock formation. Red and Rhidian closed their eyes. Even though he believed Caleb and Alba, Red still wasn't fully convinced to walk right into the stones. They braced for impact... but when they opened them again, found themselves standing at the foot of a long, sweeping flight of steps. Alba blew out the lantern because they didn't need it; the whole place was brightly lit. There were flaming stakes, intermittently placed each side of the staircase, which made the scene appear as a medieval fortress. The steps were solid marble and reflected the flickering flames from the burning torches.

'See? Told you,' Caleb said; the smug look on his face was annoying.

'What happens now?' Red just about had time to finish his question when there was movement at the top. Suddenly two figures appeared – both were really tall and stacked like marble pillars. They were clad in body armour.

'I guess that is that,' Rhidian conceded. 'We're not going to get past them.'

'What? Giving up already, Rhidian?' Caleb said in a condescending tone.

'How can we possibly overcome those two?' Rhidian said; the reality of it seemed ominous.

'Like the stones, Rhidian. It's only an illusion,' Alba interjected.

'They sure look real enough to me,' Red added.

'That's the whole point, isn't it?' Caleb rounded.

'So, you're saying they can't harm us?' Rhidian asked honestly.

'I didn't say that,' Caleb retorted.

'What? They *can* harm us?' Red and Rhidian piped up.

'If you believe that they are real, then yes,' Caleb said.

'You have to believe that they are an illusion, and no harm will come to you,' Alba said. He looked at the two of them, and they appeared confused and fearful. 'Look, if Caleb and I show you how to handle this situation, you can follow our lead.' His eyes were wide when he explained. The engineer and Red nodded reluctantly.

'Right, follow me.' Caleb began to climb the marble steps, closely followed by Alba. Rhidian and Red walked a couple of steps behind the sorcerers. Rhidian looked up and he could clearly see the two guards.

Up close, the two figures were a formidable sight, much more so than farther away and that was bad enough.

'They've got to be at least seven-foot-tall, Caleb,' Rhidian gasped.

'Hold your nerve,' Alba said without taking his eyes from the beasts. The giants didn't have any recognisable features. If they had faces then the visors they wore obscured them. The guards' bodies were completely clad in smooth armour – from top-to-toe. They weren't like the medieval knights from those old stories. Those were dressed in clumsy metal plates with gaps and joints. No, these two were in white, glistening, body-hugging combat gear with a smooth outer layer. Each stood firm and appeared human in shape, but GIGANTIC.

The guards were parallel to each other and held a large spear-like weapon, but with a blade instead of a spike. The blade started from the middle of the shaft (slightly above the guard's grip) and ended at the top. It looked terrifying, like a huge scythe. They could obviously see the wizards as they approached – why hadn't they moved down the steps to intercept the enemy?

Caleb stepped up first, quickly followed by Alba. Rhidian and Red had a better view of the entrance from up here. Beyond the guards was a huge pair of marble doors, which looked as though they weighed a ton.

'Well, this is the scary part,' Caleb's voice echoed, as he took a couple of steps towards the entrance. He stopped when the sentinels automatically moved into a battle stance. The ground shook when they stamped their right foot down. Also, a cloud of dust flittered through the air. The soldiers had been dormant for a very long time.

'Caleb,' Red's soft voice echoed. 'Forgive me for saying, but if they're illusions, why did the ground vibrate when they stamped on it?'

'Yeah, surely there wouldn't have been any sound from a projection?' Rhidian cut in.

'They have a point,' Alba confessed.

'Maybe we'll need to rethink this whole situation,' Caleb agreed.

'Rethink? What are you talking about? I thought you'd had this all sown up,' Rhidian said, and the panic was evident. Without anyone realising it, Red, built up some courage and walked to Caleb's side. He peered at the two statues. The dust had mostly settled, but the guardians hadn't moved another inch.

'What are you doing, Red?' Caleb asked, without looking down.

'Honestly, I don't know,' he said, but walked past the wizard and when Caleb went to grab his arm, the youngster pulled away.

'Red, what are you doing? Get back here,' Rhidian insisted. 'They'll kill you, you idiot,' he rasped.

'Hold on,' Alba interrupted.

'Why?' Rhidian bit back. 'He's going to die at any second.'

'Because the guards aren't attacking him, see?' Caleb added, and he was right. Red was walking slowly towards the giants but they hadn't moved to stop him.

'What's happening?' Rhidian called out, concerned.

'I don't know,' Caleb reacted, as he watched the boy get closer to them. But Red was the only one who wasn't panicking. In fact, it was the calmest he'd felt in quite a long time. He eventually stopped in between the two solid beings. He looked up and swept a glance from side-to-side. Rhidian was almost bursting.

'R-Red, c-come back,' he stammered.

'No, let him do what he's doing,' Caleb insisted. Alba turned to Rhidian and nodded in compliance with his fellow wizard. Red continued walking between the two figures and closer to the doors. Everyone looked on in anticipation. The guards still didn't move as Red approached the colossal entrance. Then a strange thing happened – the doors cracked open!

'Oh my God,' Rhidian said, his mouth wide. Then, Red turned to face his companions. The granite slabs slowly scraped across the ground and created a fan effect pattern in the grey dust. Eventually, the doors came to a stop – the sound boomed throughout the cavern.

'Let them through,' Red said in a calm voice. He looked much older for a moment.

'You heard the boy. Let's go,' Caleb said and moved off. Alba and Rhidian watched as the wizard walked between the guards and beyond. The two sentinels didn't flinch. Now it was Alba and Rhidian's turn.

'Come on, you'll be fine,' Red assured them. Shocked, they listened to the boy and nervously edged through the gap. Red smiled and turned to look at what awaited them beyond the doorway. The scene was lit in exactly the same way as the steps they'd just climbed. They were lost for words when they saw the huge mountain of marble steps. They each stood mesmerised for a moment, until a noise of grinding stone brought them back to reality. The guards were returning to their original position. The doors began to close.

'We have to go,' Caleb said. And all four of them walked through and stood at the base of the vast stairway. The grinding of stone against stone silenced when the doors finally closed.

'Well, there's no going back now,' Red chirped up.

'Never mind that. What on earth did you do, young man?' Rhidian questioned.

'We don't need to bother the boy right now, Rhidian,' Alba said. 'We've a lot of steps to climb.'

'But...' Rhidian was about to say.

'Come on, or we'll leave you behind,' Red joked, and Caleb chuckled too.

Chapter 27
The Horizon

The sheer scope of the steps seemed endless. Rhidian was burning up with questions to ask Red. Caleb and Alba looked so calm as they plodded on with every lift and drop. The engineer continued climbing, but eventually had to stop. His legs were burning and his back ached.

'Hold on,' Rhidian finally spoke up. 'I need to rest for a short while.' He sounded out of breath too.

'Okay, if we must,' Caleb muttered.

'Come on, Caleb, I'm tired too,' Alba said in agreement with Rhidian.

'I could go on forever,' Red added with a grin.

'Bloody youngsters,' Rhidian joked, and sat down on a step. They took in water and whatever food they had left. 'No!' Rhidian broke the silence while eating.

'No? No what?' Caleb retorted.

'No, I can't go any further until someone explains what happened with Red earlier,' he demanded.

'Quite simply, I don't know,' Alba said, and he looked as if he were telling the truth.

'I don't know how I did it, either,' Red said.

'It's as if those stone thingies *knew* you.' Rhidian furrowed his brow, his beady eyes locked on to Red's. 'Caleb, do you have any answers?'

'Same as you – I've no idea,' Caleb responded.

'But you must have some clue?' Rhidian probed.

'I don't speculate unless I have all the facts,' he replied, not giving away any more. Rhidian sat in silence. He realised that he wasn't going to get any information out of these guys.

'Are we all rested?' Red said and lazily looked across to the others. There were nods from everyone. 'Let's go,' he said, with a shrug of the shoulders.

Rhidian eventually got to his feet. Everything ached, but when he looked at Alba, realised that *he* must be feeling a lot worse. So, Rhidian shook it off and the first few steps were always the hardest. The tops of his legs were stiff and his calves also still burned. He gazed upwards and rolled his shoulders. He took a deep breath and winced. The others were already a few steps ahead and the incline looked more like a cliff-face than a flight of stairs… it was daunting.

He pushed it to the back of his mind and focussed. He moved a little faster in order to catch up with the others. Red was leading, with Caleb behind and Alba shadowed them. Rhidian had already calculated that they'd been climbing for half an hour or so. They all continued and must have looked like ants on the vast staircase to the stars.

'I see the top!' Red shouted, his voice rich with excitement.

'Great,' Caleb mumbled. Alba couldn't even speak, but with Rhidian beside him, gave him the strength to continue walking. They finally reached the plateau. By the time Alba and Rhidian arrived, they saw Red and Caleb standing like the statues they'd passed earlier. And the reason for that was the huge sight that greeted them.

'Wow, it's a ship – *The Horizon*,' Rhidian gasped, whilst reading the nameplate. Floating before them was a large vessel, docked on a cliff edge. The sight of the magnificent ship took the engineer's breath away. 'How on earth did it get here?' He looked around and couldn't see a way into the cave.

'Wow.' Red looked on in awe.

'That is an awesome feat of engineering and craftsmanship,' Rhidian said, and walked right up to the edge of the jetty and touched it, as if it was an old friend.

'It is a sight to behold,' Caleb responded.

'What's it doing here?' Alba asked as he gazed at the sheer size.

'I've no idea,' Rhidian said, shaking his head.

The whole vessel was the size of a sports field. It had a central building, riddled with different rooms on two floors. There were no zeppelin-like balloons aloft the vessel. All the lift they needed was placed neatly underneath, just like on the supply ship.

'I'm still trying to figure out how it got in here. It's a sealed cavern in the mountain,' Rhidian said with a puzzled look.

'That's an illusion. Probably to stop anyone snooping from above,' Alba said.

'What? The same as the rocks hiding the entrance?' Rhidian assumed and Alba nodded. 'So it must have been brought here by a wizard.'

'Do you think that Obsidian took it from Valusha and owns it now?' Red asked.

'Yes, he does,' came a voice from behind them.

They all turned to come face-to-face with the figure of an old man. He was tall and slim. His eyes were the deepest blue and were perfectly framed inside round spectacles. His skin was weathered and filled with deep lines. Under his nose was a thick grey moustache, which seemed to have a life of its own. Under his bottom lip, another small patch of grey in a triangular shape. Obsidian also had a great mop of sweeping, white hair, exactly the same colour as the 'tache and soul patch. He wore ordinary everyday clothes – a plain blue shirt and a pair of tan, corduroy trousers ending in brown boots.

All four of them stood, almost glued to the spot. This was the person they'd travelled all this way to find. It was a breath-taking moment. For once, no one knew what to say. It had taken so long to find this great leader and at times they thought they'd never make it. Rhidian, of the entire group, decided to say something.

'A-are you really Obsidian?' Rhidian stammered, his bottom lip trembling.

'I am. And who might you be? And what are you doing here?' came the wizard's sharp reply.

'I'm really glad to meet you, sir.' Rhidian replied meekly. 'I'm an engineer and I fix and build stuff on Valusha. Well, I did.'

'We've come to find *you*,' Caleb cut in, a little annoyed with the lukewarm reception they were getting.

'Yes, a long way too,' Alba uttered.

'And we lost a good friend along the way,' Red added, the sadness still in his voice.

'Nonsense,' Obsidian snapped back.

'What do you mean *nonsense*? You don't know anything,' Rhidian responded; he felt really annoyed. He was beginning not to like this person, but changed his mind in an instant.

'Because I'm here.' The familiar voice of Rebus reverberated around them. Everyone took their focus from Obsidian and looked towards the other end of the platform, from which, out of the shadows came their companion; he looked good. The air seemed charged with electricity as they all surged towards the wizard and surrounded him. There were hugs and smiles, hoots and cheers.

'How did you ever survive that river?' Alba asked totally in disbelief.

'That was all down to Obsidian. If he hadn't found me, then it would have been a totally different story,' Rebus said gratefully. 'I've told him everything by the way.'

'Yes, and by the sounds of it we've a massive task ahead,' Obsidian said with a serious refrain.

'So, you'll go back?' Alba interjected.

'Yes, old friend, I will,' Obsidian responded and hugged the old wizard. 'I've been away far too long,' he said as he broke away from the embrace.

'I wondered if you'd remembered me, master,' Alba gushed.

'How could I forget you, Alba?' He smiled.

'If you don't mind me asking, Obsidian, how did you escape?' Rhidian asked.

'Isn't it obvious?' the ancient wizard answered, and gestured towards the ship. 'I took it. Well, originally it was mine to begin with.'

'Wow, that was sneaky, to steal that from under the nose of the mighty Jenta-Lor,' Red chuckled.

'Well it wasn't easy, but I managed to get it to fly, and used my magic when I got far enough away from Valusha.' When he said it, he dropped back in thought to his beloved city, just for a moment. He then blinked his eyes and shook off the old memory. 'Let's get some food, drink and rest. We've a lot to catch up on,' he said to Alba and Rebus. 'Once we've done that, I've something to show *all* of you later,' he continued, and winked. 'Come, follow me, there is much to see.'

The wizard turned and walked away from the jetty. The others didn't waste any time and followed their master from the docking bay and up yet another flight of steps.

Obsidian had created a vast mansion inside the rock formation of the mountain. It appeared as a grand palace. As they followed, each tried to take in the amazing splendour of their surroundings. Obsidian wasn't one for small measures. There was marble everywhere and high glossy pillars.

'Come, come, don't dawdle,' the old wizard's voice echoed from further in. And everyone did as they were asked.

Chapter 28
The Arrival

After their meal, Obsidian led them to another vast room. This one resembled a museum. It had large circular pillars, which reached up to a high ceiling, and a wide, glossy marble floor. The marble floor had deep gouges and a network of claw marks. They all looked, but no one mentioned it (not wanting to appear awkward).

At the farthest end of the hall was a huge open window, as high as it was wide, and a bright light emitted from beyond that. The blinding white light engulfed the whole of the inside of the room. Not only that, but the air was filled with an almost ear-splitting rush of water. This room was cooler too, because air wafted in from outside.

'What is that?' Rebus asked in a raised voice, wincing as he said it.

'That, my friend, is a waterfall,' Obsidian revealed.

'So, that leads to the outside of the mountain?' Rhidian said.

'Yes,' Obsidian responded. 'It's the waterfall that keeps this place hidden.'

'Ingenious,' Alba said with a grin.

'Have you thought of sealing it off?' Caleb joined in the conversation. 'Just to cut down on the noise,' Caleb added, his eyes creased.

'There's a reason why I haven't,' Obsidian added.

'And what's that?' Rebus pressed, but as he said it, there was a sound that came from the other side of the waterfall. The sound cut through the rush of heavy water. The intermittent, deep rich sound of thulump-thulump-thulump. Added to that, as the pumping got closer and closer, a searing shriek ripped through the air. The high-pitched squeal got louder. Obsidian stood calmly by as everyone else braced themselves. In a swift moment, the curtain of white water was breached and in swooped a *DRAGON*! None had ever seen the likes of it before, and their first instinct was to get right out of there. Obsidian saw their terror.

'Don't be afraid, he's a friend,' the master wizard spoke calmly.

The colossal creature landed on the glassy, marble floor and skidded a few metres, tearing new lines, before it came to a stop in front of Obsidian. Now the grooves in the marble made more sense.

'Everyone, I'd like you to meet Shard,' the wizard announced. At first, no one knew quite what to say; they just gawped at him. Even Red was lost for words.

Shard was at least six metres high, maybe even taller. The colour tone of his skin was an inky-blue, which made the creature look majestic. The wings, now safely folded away, could open to a twelve-metre wingspan. His head had a long, narrow snout and above that – two translucent blue eyes. On top of its forehead, a pair of antennae, which probably helped its balance as it glided through the air. Further down Shard's armour-plated body were its hind legs. These two tree-trunks could easily power the beast into flight on the shortest of lift-offs. Below them, it had long talons at the end of its feet. It appeared beautiful, but so powerful it could probably tear a human in half in a split-second and even a wizard come to that.

Something really strange happened in the next instant. Red tentatively walked towards the giant beast. Obsidian looked bemused by the youngster, but said nothing. Caleb, Alba and Rhidian had seen him do this previously with the guards and said nothing to hinder the teenager. Red walked right up to the dragon and put out his hand to touch its scales. Another really weird thing took place. The dragon calmly dropped its head and allowed Red to stroke its nose. Obsidian witnessed this and didn't know how to react. Rebus was bewildered but strangely happy.

'What are you doing, boy?' Obsidian asked.

'I-I don't know, but it feels natural,' Red admitted. He felt calm and unafraid – exactly as he'd experienced earlier. He didn't know why.

'This is very significant. Shard has never lowered his head to anyone.' Obsidian gasped and then a thought filled the wizard's mind. He announced with great grandeur, 'You are a wizard.'

'W-what? No, that's impossible,' Rhidian reacted. 'How can that be? He's just a boy.'

'It's perfectly true, Rhidian. Red is a wizard,' Rebus revealed.

'I knew he was a wizard,' Caleb said, his eyes flashed with excitement.

'Me too,' Alba agreed. 'Well, I had an inkling. The way in which he dealt with those guards.'

'I knew you knew something,' Rhidian retorted.

'I wondered how you all got past those,' Obsidian queried.

'B-but, I don't think I'm a wizard,' Red protested. He didn't understand any of this.

'This is a lot to take in, Red, and I totally understand your confusion. I know nothing about wizards and their powers, but you do seem to have something special,' Rhidian explained as best as he could.

Red suddenly broke away from the dragon and ran out of the room. Rhidian was about to go after him when Rebus spoke up.

'Let him go, Rhidian. It's a lot for the boy to understand.' Rebus nodded towards Rhidian, who nodded back in compliance.

'This changes everything,' Caleb announced. 'We have a dragon now. Can Shard belch fire?'

'Uh oh, I don't know, Caleb. I must go and talk to the boy,' Obsidian insisted, and left the room in search of Red.

'This is all very confusing.' Rhidian sighed and looked into Rebus' eyes. 'I'm really happy you're alive, old friend.'

'Me, too,' Rebus said with a smile.

'I think we'd all better go back to the hall to mull this over. What do you all say?' Alba asked.

'Yeah, I'm with you,' Rhidian agreed.

'Me too,' Rebus said.

'Yep, let's go,' Caleb added.

'What about... you know, the elephant in the room?' Rhidian said, with a nod of the head.

'He's not an elephant, Rhidian, he's a...' But before Caleb could mock any further, Rhidian looked at him and laughed.

'Come on, you lot. Let Shard alone for now,' Rebus chuckled.

'Elephant, indeed,' Alba mused.

Obsidian found Red in the corridor and walked over to the confused lad. He sat next to him on a smooth plinth.

'Look, I know this must be hard for you to understand,' Obsidian said sympathetically. 'I was born into it and I still find it weird.'

'Really?' Red finally responded.

'Oh yes, it was a learning curve all right.'

'I have been getting strange feelings for a while, but I tried to stop thinking about it,' Red admitted.

'Firstly, you have to try to understand them, and then let them embrace your heart – I can teach you,' Obsidian encouraged.

'Would you?' Red gushed. He felt he could relay his feelings more freely to the ancient wizard.

'Of course. Us wizards have to stick together. It won't all come easily, but you will eventually learn how to read and understand your powers,' he said, and that made Red feel a lot less scared. 'Come on, let's join the others. We've a lot to discuss.'

Chapter 29
The Flight

It was the early hours and Red couldn't sleep. He got out of bed and got dressed. He made his way down the cold stone steps to the Great Hall. The room was lit by flaming torches, which lined the outside of the room. The soft glow and crackle of the flame spat a whisper in the dark corners.

Red leaned up against the door and gave it a little nudge. The door opened but nothing stirred and all he could hear was the loud hiss of flowing water. Breathing hard, the boy gingerly made his way inside. His eyes took some time to adjust to the yellow flames, until he made out a large black silhouette to one side of the vast cavern.

Shard didn't give any clue as to being spied on. Red stood... and didn't move for some time. He gazed in overwhelming awe at the beauty and sheer size of the dragon. In this light, the scales appeared the deepest shade of blue, almost black. Red could see the belly rise and fall as the beast took shallow breaths. He wanted to touch him again, to feel the power and the warmth. The young wizard ran his tongue along his lips and swallowed – his mouth was still dry from sleep. It was so weird; he'd never really thought about dragons before and here he was with an urge to be with him. He felt as though he was a chunk of iron being pulled towards a huge magnet.

He walked closer; the ground vibrated underfoot at Shard's breathing. This gave Red's stomach an excited tingle. Red's eyes were completely adjusted to the light and he could see the whole outline of the beast. He got bolder and stretched out to touch the dragon's belly. He had to make sure not to step on the giant's huge talons. Shard's left eye suddenly flickered open and Red, in mid-stretch, gasped and pulled back.

Shard lifted his head and stared directly at the boy. Red froze to the spot.

'I-I didn't me-an any h-arm,' he trembled, but the dragon did nothing... only kept his eye trained on him; all the time his breathing stayed shallow. The dragon opened his mouth and Red opened his too, to shout for help, but a garbled, high-pitched squeaked hissed out.

'Don't worry, little one, I won't hurt you,' the dragon spoke, in a deep, soothing tone. Red almost choked.

'Y-you can sp-eak?' Red struggled to get the words to work. 'Th-at's amazing.' The boy's legs suddenly felt like jelly and he didn't know how to react.

'Of course, don't all dragons?' Shard answered flippantly.

'I don't know. You're the first one I've ever seen... never mind spoken to,' Red admitted, and still looked totally shell-shocked.

'I'm going to get up. You'd better step back,' the dragon warned. 'I'm stiff after being asleep in the same position for so long. I need to flex my wings. Would you like to come for a ride?' Shard asked. Red opened his mouth to speak again, but this time nothing came out. 'Is that a no?' Shard demanded, seeming a little hurt.

'No...err, I mean, yes, err, of course I would love to come for a ride with you,' Red stumbled. 'I've never ridden a dragon before.' Red's eyes were wide and his mouth was even wider.

'That's no problem,' Shard said, and climbed up onto all fours; the sound of his claws gave a piercing screech against the smooth granite floor. Red craned his neck to take in the whole sight. The beast was spectacular. Shard made his way to the rush of the water. He stepped up onto the wide opening and unfurled his wings. He had his back to the boy so he slowly turned his head towards Red. He then lowered his left wing, making a kind of slope onto his back. 'Well, are you coming or not?' the dragon insisted.

'Coming... definitely coming with you,' Red answered quickly. He scuttled along the floor until he was close to the tip of the dragon's wing. He gingerly stepped up and, as lightly as he could, walked to the animal's shoulder. Underfoot felt solid and awkward, like an uneven stone path. Red expected it to be all soft and feathery, like a bird's.

'Don't worry about hurting me, young man. I'm pretty rugged.'

'It's Red. My name is Red,' Red repeated.

'Okay, Red, great to meet you,' Shard conveyed the greeting. 'You can get comfortable on my neck. Grab a firm grip of my scales and we can take flight.' Red was beside himself with excitement and fear. He settled astride the dragon's neck and grabbed hold of two protruding scales. He held on so tight that his knuckles whitened. 'Ready?' Shard asked.

'Yep,' Red answered reluctantly, but it was too late to worry now. Shard set his wings in position and began a gallop towards the icy white of the waterfall. As they approached the deafening curtain of water, Red clenched his eyes shut. He almost lost grip when he felt the ice-cold rush of water on his body. But it soon turned to cold wind and the canter to a glide. He opened his eyes... he was flying! The water dripped from his sodden hair and rolled down his face and chin. The boy blinked his eyes to release the excess.

'You all right, Red?' Shard called out, but as Red was about to answer, the dragon dropped down the side of the cliff-face, at an alarming angle – the speed was immense. Red's mouth was filled with freezing cold air, which stabbed the back of his throat like a dagger. He held on with the tightest grip he could. The sun was coming up on the horizon and illuminated their descent. All Red could hear was the rush of wind and the ocean, which was closing in. He tried again to call out, but it was futile.

Shard picked up speed and headed straight for the body of water. As he got within ten metres, he lifted his head and swooped parallel to the surface of the sea, but Red had closed his eyes again long before then. The boy could feel lift again and when he did finally reopen his eyes could see the golden horizon melt into view. It was an amazing vista.

The dragon tilted this way and that, swooping in between rocks and gorges, dipping down and lifting up to a peak. The fear soon evaporated and Red was enjoying every movement. It was so natural to him and he found himself actually guiding the dragon. Shard gave in to the subtle commands of a tug to the left or a pull to the right. Red was now a Dragon Rider.

Chapter 30
The Plan

Over the next week or so, Red went out on numerous flights with Shard and proved to be a natural at piloting a dragon. They were becoming inseparable too. Obsidian also took the boy under his wing and taught him the fundamentals of wizardry. He told the boy that if they took back Valusha then he would give him proper lessons. Caleb also said that he would help him with his magic when back in the city.

Alba, with rest and food, soon regained his strength and was back to his old self and that's what everyone was waiting for. He imparted his wisdom on the young wizard so Red had a wealth of knowledge all around him. There were many meetings, especially with Rebus and Obsidian, and the tension was at a high when, one evening, Obsidian summoned everyone to the Great Hall, which had changed.

It was still as grand a place as all the other rooms in the world Obsidian had created, but instead of the open floor, which led to the waterfall at the other end, now, it held a large granite dining table. Obsidian was already sitting at one end, with chairs laid out to each side. Everyone filed in. Obsidian had sent Red to deliver the message. Things were so unusual here that no one thought anything different of there being a banquet table, which wasn't there before. After everyone was seated, Obsidian spoke.

'In order to take back Valusha, we must have a plan,' he said sensibly; there were nods all around.

'So,' Rhidian spoke up, 'what is it?'

'Well, let's look at the reality-side of things,' Rebus added.

'Such as?' Alba asked with interest.

'We're not only attacking Jenta-Lor and his police force,' Obsidian said seriously. 'There are lots of innocent people to think about.' Rhidian immediately thought about his wife, Mia.

'Where did he recruit his police force?' Caleb asked in curiosity.

'In truth, no one knows,' Obsidian said. 'One minute they weren't there, the next they were. He'd also convinced the people to vote me out. He must hold very persuasive powers,' the ancient wizard added.

'You can't just recruit random people and train them up into soldiers in the blink of an eye,' Rhidian reasoned.

'No, and that's why I think that Jenta-Lor is not a mortal!' Rebus commented.

'*Not* a mortal? What are you saying, Rebus?' Rhidian pressed.

'What Rebus is saying, Rhidian, is that Jenta-Lor is a wizard!' Caleb said.

'So, what does this mean?' Red enquired.

'It means the lying, cheating…' Obsidian stopped before he got too angry. 'Well, it means we're dealing with a very cunning individual. One who has used magic to take over by telling everyone in Valusha that wizards are evil creatures. His so-called police force must only be the poor souls who have been brainwashed into working for him. Vulnerable citizens of Valusha who are now his "zombie army",' the wizard concluded.

'We'll have to prove that theory,' Caleb said.

'And that means that this "damper field" that is supposed to be expelling magic from being used in Valusha is actually created by a *wizard*. And is, in fact, allowing Jenta-Lor to practise magic inside the city, whilst stopping enemy wizards from getting back in,' Obsidian concluded.

'It all sounds full-proof,' Rhidian stated. 'How are we even going to get near enough to breakdown this damper field?' Rhidian continued with urgency.

'I think I know a way to collapse the field from the inside,' Obsidian announced.

'So, what's the plan?' Red asked eagerly, and the others looked intrigued too.

'From the *inside*? How?' Caleb was sceptical. 'There is no one left inside Valusha who can help us. I think I was the last one to escape,' he said.

'No, there is one more inside Valusha that can help us. But that person doesn't even know that they are a wizard,' Obsidian said, and he rested his chin on his clenched hands and stared into the distance.

'But magic can't be used on the inside *because* of the damper field, so how is this person going to use their power?' Caleb questioned.

'If we can distract Jenta-Lor enough to take his mind off the field, it will weaken, and that's when we can strike. The wizard can then use their power from within,' Obsidian said with confidence.

'Is that possible?' Alba appeared as if he were in two minds.

'Think about it, Alba. Jenta-Lor has to use his magic power for the damper field and the mind control that he's probably got on the people. And he'll have to use his magic to stop our attack. Something has got to give to juggle all that lot, and I don't think he's powerful enough to do all that. So our wizard can then break down the field.'

'That sounds about right,' Caleb agreed with a nod.

'Who is this person?' Rebus asked; even he didn't know.

'I've kept this a secret for a long time and I'm not about to reveal it right now. You'll all know when the time comes. I need to get within a short distance of that person to contact them. If they can then shut down the damper field, then I think the army will dissolve with it, leaving Jenta-Lor exposed to attack,' Obsidian said.

'There are lots of innocent people in that city, including my wife,' Rhidian said, his eyes sad. 'If Jenta-Lor is as unscrupulous as you say he is, then what is stopping him from using the innocent as a barrier and sacrificing them?' Rhidian explained, and almost broke down.

'Nothing. And he will use them to shield his army, but we'll have to use the element of surprise. We'll have to attack at night and take him down before he even knows we're there,' Obsidian spoke, and looked at his faithful companions.

'When do we go?' Caleb said.

'We start our journey at midday, that is if you're feeling up to it, Alba?' Obsidian answered.

'I'm fine now, thank you, Obsidian,' Alba said.

'We have a ship and there are six of us,' Rebus said in a raised voice. But before he could say anything else, there was the familiar flapping of giant wings. All eyes instinctively peered at the waterfall and Shard came bursting through, but not at such a pace that he couldn't stop. He gracefully skidded to a halt, metres from the table, water droplets flying in all directions. Everyone except Obsidian took a sharp intake of breath. Red just smiled at the spectacle. Shard composed himself. He folded away his wings and his breathing eased. He stooped down until his whole body was in a comfortable position and there was a pause; no one spoke for a moment or two, and then…

'I am also coming on this journey,' the dragon announced. Nearly everyone was astounded, including Obsidian; all except Red, who already knew the dragon could speak.

'Shard,' Obsidian gushed, 'you can speak and understand.'

'Everything you've ever said to me,' the dragon admitted.

'B-but, why didn't you tell me?' Obsidian asked.

'One day I was going to tell you, and that day is now,' Shard said simply.

'What made you want to talk?' Obsidian probed.

'Once a dragon finds a rider, then that person becomes his companion and that's when we speak,' Shard said with pride.

'He spoke to me first,' Red piped up with a tremble.

'You truly are the Dragon Rider,' Obsidian said with pride. 'Now let us eat and prepare for the journey.' Food appeared on the table in front of them. It was their last meal in Gelbar.

'I propose a toast,' Obsidian announced. 'Hail the Dragon Rider,' the wizard said as he raised his glass, and the other noticed there were glasses of wine sitting in front of them too. So, glasses were raised all around.

'Seven of us it is then,' Rebus gushed.

'I was hoping you'd come along, Shard. Thank you,' Obsidian said with gratitude.

*****

When the meal was over, everyone got on board *The Horizon*. Red unhitched the last of the tethers and soon the ship departed the dock. From the jetty, it looked as though it was heading straight for the sun as it rose up high. The air was warm and the wind calm. The spectacle looked amazing. *The Horizon*, which was piloted by Rhidian, sailed majestically across the summer sky as Shard flew parallel. Red gazed across and admired the beauty of the creature as it gracefully floated on a current of warm air. But this was just the beginning – the start of a journey which no one knew the outcome.

Chapter 31
Damper Field

The journey took two days and luckily they hadn't encountered any pirate ships on the way. Obsidian asked Rhidian to prepare to slow the engines and bring the vessel to a stop. It was approaching evening and they could just about make out Valusha in the distance through the twilight haze.

'We'll have to wait until it's completely dark before we even attempt to approach the city,' Obsidian said. Caleb and Rebus were on the deck and were soon joined by Alba. Red was talking to Shard to the rear of the ship – there was plenty of space for the dragon to stretch out and rest on the deck.

'So, what's the attack plan?' Rhidian asked as he eased back on the revs. *The Horizon* finally came gently to a halt. It tilted and rocked slightly as it settled.

'Come on, let's join the others out there and work out a way to take back Valusha without hurting the innocent,' Obsidian said, as he made his way out of the control room. He turned to the stern and called the others to follow. There, next to

Shard and Red, everyone gathered and waited for the wise one to speak. It was a warm evening and quite pleasant; that would have been great if it wasn't for the fact that they were about to go into battle.

'This is not going to be easy,' Obsidian said with conviction. 'The biggest problem we have to face is the fact that Jenta-Lor will feel us coming. I'm sure he'll be ready to fight. He's not going to give up his position as ruler if he can help it. He'll probably use any force necessary to prevent us from taking over. We have to restore order. Any ideas?'

'He's got the damper field too, and that's our first challenge,' Rebus spoke up. 'You said you've a contact inside that can help us, Obsidian?'

'What if we create our own damper field before we get within range so Jenta-Lor won't feel us coming?' Alba said. Everyone looked at the old wizard in complete surprise.

'Great idea, Alba,' Caleb said with excitement.

'Then, when we're close enough, I can use my "mind transfer" to try and contact our ally inside the city.' Obsidian looked deep in thought.

'I'm a little sceptical on one thing,' Caleb added. Obsidian broke away from his focus and nodded politely.

'What worries you?' the wise sorcerer enquired.

'Why doesn't Jenta-Lor know about this wizard who is living among his people?' Caleb queried. 'Surely he can sense that person too?'

'Oh, that's easy,' Obsidian said with a polite smile. 'The wizard in question doesn't know they have magical powers. I made sure of that before I left. So if the wizard doesn't know they're a wizard, then neither will Jenta-Lor.'

There was silence for a moment as the others paused for thought.

'Brilliant!' Red gushed.

'So who is this person?' Rebus asked, the curiosity too strong.

'I can't say at the moment. There are a lot of things riding on this… it's complicated and very flimsy. I'm hoping that this person is still in Valusha,' he shrugged his shoulders. 'I don't even know if the person in question is married and if the wizard has a family. If they have, then maybe they won't want to risk hurting them,' Obsidian admitted. 'My feeling is that my contact is still there; it's a risk I'm willing to take. What about you?' He looked at all the others. 'Are you still with me?' There was quiet thought and then everyone nodded in compliance. 'Okay. We have other things to sort first. Right, this damper field, let's put that in place,' Obsidian said.

'We'll need all our concentration to conjure the field. So, if we sit in a circle on the floor,' Obsidian said, 'let's sit on the deck and link minds.' All the wizards sat, including Red. Rhidian stepped back.

'Come, sit next to me,' Shard said to the engineer, who was beginning to feel like a third wheel. The dragon gestured with his eyes towards a wooden barrel that was secured next to him. 'We don't want to interrupt their little magical games, do we?' he said, which made Rhidian smile.

While the sorcerers conducted their experiment, Rhidian turned to Shard.

'I sense something is troubling you, Rhidian?' Shard said, getting directly to the point.

'Well.' Rhidian then lowered his voice so that the wizards couldn't hear. 'It's about what's going to take place,' he said, and the concern was evident in his mannerisms.

'Yes,' Shard said and turned his large head in Rhidian's direction.

'Make no bones about it, but we're going into battle.' Shard didn't interrupt and let the engineer speak. 'At some point, you and Red will face a lot of danger.' Shard could hear the anxiety in his voice.

'Go on,' Shard nodded.

'Look, I've grown very fond of Red. He feels like a son to me and I would hate anything to happen to him.' Rhidian said the words and Shard could see and hear the emotion.

'I totally understand, Rhidian,' Shard retorted, 'and I will do my utmost to keep him safe… but we are going into war. And that brings with it all kinds of scary situations. But Red is a *wizard,* Rhidian, and wizards have an uncanny way of surviving. Don't underestimate the young lad,' Shard said, and gave a friendly nod. Rhidian smiled and then turned away to witness the ritual of the bonding of wizards.

'It's done,' Alba exclaimed.

'Now he won't feel *us* coming, and we'll have the element of surprise,' Caleb said excitedly.

*****

Evening eventually drew in and it became dark enough for the crew to start up *The Horizon* and head towards the city of Valusha.

'If we dock on the south side, where *this* ship was originally tethered, then we can get in without being seen,' Obsidian said sensibly.

'Brilliant,' Rebus gushed. 'They won't be expecting us there. In fact, they won't be expecting us at all!'

'Okay, good plan,' Caleb and Alba agreed. Rhidian and Red nodded in unison.

'We'll still have to cut the engines as we approach, just in case there is someone on watch,' Rhidian announced.

'Good thinking, Rhidian,' Obsidian said with a grin.

'Oh, that's not good,' Rhidian exclaimed as he pointed in the distance.

'What is it?' Red asked with interest.

'There's a fog,' Rhidian chirped up. 'That's going to make things a bit more tricky, but it'll also help mask our arrival.'

The inky-blue night sky soon became enveloped in a thick, grey mist.

'It won't matter so much about hiding now. We can go directly to Jenta-Lor's palace and confront him head-on, instead of sneaking up on him.'

'But it's going to be a problem to manoeuvre through the mist,' Rhidian said.

'I can help with that,' Shard said in a deep voice. 'I can navigate in bad weather conditions. I've done it before.'

'That's cool,' Rhidian said. 'That'll help a lot.'

'You're amazing,' Red gushed and gave a wide grin.

'Start the engines, Rhidian,' Obsidian commanded. 'Head for the palace. Here we go.'

Chapter 32
Silent Attack

The grey mist came in wisps at first and began to settle its tentacles on the vessel like a sleepy snake. Soon *The Horizon* was engulfed in a dense fog and Rhidian had to slow right down.

'Shut off the engines and coast,' Obsidian said to Rhidian. The engineer felt like saying something like "Aye-aye, Captain", but thought better of it.

'Okay, Shard, you're up,' Rhidian said.

Red was on the deck with the dragon, where he'd been since the start of the journey. In fact, they were inseparable. Rebus, Alba and Caleb were standing at the bow, holding onto the rail and peered silently into the mist. It was eerie. All that could be heard were the sounds of the timbers creaking and groaning as if in pain.

Shard lifted his head and his blue eyes seemed to glow as he concentrated.

'This is unnerving,' Red whispered.

'I suppose so,' Shard retorted, his voice deep and rich. 'Rhidian, keep on the course you're already on. It's not far now, maybe just under a mile ahead,' Shard relayed the information.

Soon they could all make out the glowing lights of Valusha and Obsidian felt a pang in his stomach. So did the others, especially Rhidian; Mia was somewhere within those lights. He hoped she was safe and no harm had come to her since he'd been abducted.

'Steady, Rhidian, just a little to the right if you please,' Shard instructed.

Through the swirls of mist they could plainly see Jenta-Lor's palace. It was high above everything else in the city and lit in a plethora of colours. There was complete silence on the deck.

'I'll make contact with—' but Obsidian didn't have time to finish his words; a loud siren was raised which cut through the still night.

'There's a hive of activity down there!' Caleb shouted from the deck.

'We must have breached a sensor or something,' Obsidian winced. 'Start her up and get us out of here, now!' he shouted. 'We don't have the element of surprise any more, but we do still have the fog.'

'They're firing at us,' Alba rasped. And with that the engine turned over just as stray bullets sparked from below. Soon the ship began to lift and the shots followed.

'Take cover!' Rebus bellowed. Soon bullets were taking chunks out of the ship's hull.

'Get us out of here!' Obsidian screamed.

'I'm trying,' Rhidian said as he grappled with the wheel. 'They'll try and puncture the airbags.' But even as he said it, *The Horizon* was once again cloaked in the fog. They could hear small bangs and see flashes from below, which soon faded into the background.

Everyone urgently pooled into the control room.

'What's the plan now, master?' Rebus asked.

'Yes, our sneak attack is well and truly gone,' Caleb responded.

'It's my fault,' Obsidian said, grinding his teeth. 'I didn't give Jenta-Lor enough credit. I thought I'd have more time to connect with the wizard, but it was too quick.'

'Once this mist disappears, we'll be truly out in the open,' Alba said.

'A couple of spotlights on us and we'll be sitting ducks,' Red added.

'Rhidian, put us down somewhere safe for now. I need time to think,' Obsidian instructed.

'There are open fields to one side of the city. We'll be safe there but not for long. Shard, do you think you can find that area?' Rhidian asked.

'Yes, I can see it in the distance,' Shard replied.

'Excellent,' Obsidian said.

Soon they were away from the commotion and, through Shard's navigational skills, Rhidian steered the vessel to open flat ground. They landed with a small thud. The fog was thicker here, held by the trees and water.

'Well done, Shard,' Red squeaked excitedly.

'My pleasure,' the dragon's smooth voice retorted.

All was quiet for a while. Everyone stepped onto the deck.

'Red, you and Shard take flight and report back to us on what's happening,' Obsidian said, 'but be careful.'

'Will do,' Red said, relishing the thought of doing something important. So he climbed onto Shard's back, and they were away in a couple of heavy wing beats. Obsidian went back into the control room to forge some kind of plan with the rest of the wizards.

Rhidian stood on the deck; all he could do was steer the ship and knew nothing of battle. He closed his eyes and thought of Mia. A smile filled his face; she was beautiful. Where was she? Was she all right? She may even be close right now.

'Don't move, you are under arrest!' Rhidian blinked open his eyes and turned. He was suddenly standing toe-to-toe with a Jenta Force police officer. He could tell she was female. She stood about six foot tall and wore the usual police uniform and full-face visor, but definitely a woman's voice.

'Where on earth did you spring from?' Rhidian asked, totally surprised.

'You are under arrest,' the officer persisted and produced a set of handcuffs.

'GUYS... Rebus, Alba, Caleb... someone!' Rhidian screeched.

'Do not evade arrest,' she said in the same monotone voice. She grabbed Rhidian's wrist and was about to slap on the cuffs, when she stopped.

'W-what's happening?' Rhidian said, fully confused.

'Keep calm, Rhidian,' Obsidian said as he stepped from behind the officer. 'I've just rendered her immobile for now by a special neck grip which freezes her nerves,' he said.

'She's either a stray patrol, or there may be others,' Rhidian assumed. 'Hold on a moment,' he said and took off her visor. 'I thought I recognised that voice. It's Shana. She's a friend of my wife, but why is she a police officer for Jenta-Lor? It doesn't make any sense. She used to run a cake shop in the city. She didn't have a family and worked on her own.'

'She's been taken over with mind control. Just as I suspected,' Obsidian said. 'That would mean that Jenta-Lor's use of magic has culminated an army of officers who are just normal people. He's taken away their free will.'

'We can't attack and kill innocent people to gain control. How can we get them all out of this trance-like state?' Rebus asked with deep concern.

'I sensed the person I needed to contact was near, when we got closer to the palace. That is the only one who can break their trance, once the damper field is shut down. But I didn't have time to lock minds. I just hope that person isn't working for Jenta-Lor, or we're all doomed,' Obsidian said in anguish. 'It's a chance we have to take. Rhidian, get us airborne.' Obsidian seemed the most serious anyone had ever seen him. 'We're going back to Jenta-Lor's palace.'

'What about her?' Rhidian pointed towards the officer.

'She'll have to come with us, or she could raise the alarm,' Obsidian said sensibly. Just as they were about to lift off, Shard came to a landing on the deck.

'What's happening at the palace?' Obsidian asked the boy.

'Jenta-Lor's forces are on the ground ready for any attack,' Red said as he dismounted.

'I'll need you to distract them, without actually harming anyone,' Obsidian said. 'In fact, cause the most amount of confusion you can, but be careful because they *will* be intending to hurt you and Shard.'

'W-what? Okay.' Red was slightly confused.

'Just do as I say and we can overcome Jenta-Lor once and for all. We'll need Shard's keen eyes to navigate *The Horizon* within range of the palace again. And without being seen,' Obsidian ordered. The engines started and they lifted into the grey mist. Shana, the police officer, still in her trance, was led to safety inside the control room.

As they approached the city, still hidden by the fog, Obsidian gave the instructions. 'Kill the engines, Rhidian. Red, take Shard and cause confusion. Do anything you can.'

'What do *we* do now?' the other wizards asked.

'Nothing,' came Obsidian's reply. 'Now *I* must do something.'

'Shard, you heard what Obsidian said, as much confusion but without harming anyone,' Red pressed.

'Understood,' he replied. The great dragon swooped down as low and as fast as he could, bursting through the thinning fog. When they saw the huge beast approach, everyone on the ground ran for cover. Shard belched a trail of bright, yellow flame around the edges of the palace grounds. The utter chaos it caused pushed Jenta-Lor's soldiers away from the perimeter and close to the palace.

'At least they'll be safe bunched up together,' Red shouted in Shard's ear. Red then spotted a small compound of oil drums and indicated for Shard to concentrate his fire directly into the heart of it. The dragon belched flames which produced a large explosion and a huge fireball erupted with yellow flames and black smoke.

'Get that fire under control,' Jenta-Lor bellowed as he ran across his lawn, 'and return fire, you idiots!' he screamed. Jenta Force Police immediately responded and aimed a barrage of shots. But Shard soon swooped high up into the sky, just avoiding the spray of bullets. All was in disarray as Red looked back at the devastation he'd caused.

While all this was going on, Obsidian had knelt on the deck and connected his mind to someone inside the palace.

Chapter 33
Inside Contact

She flicked open her eyes – something had broken her away from her tortured dreams. But how was that possible? She was alone in her room. There it was again, someone calling her. There were noises outside but she was too immersed in her thoughts to care.

'Mia, you must listen to me.' Mia sat up in bed and looked around the room again. There was definitely no one in there except her and that strange voice – a voice that she seemed to recognise.

'W-who are you? Why are you messing with my mind?' Mia called out.

'Mia, you must wake up!'

'Stop it,' she said. Tears filled her eyes. 'Now go away and leave me in peace.' She reached up and put her palms to her ears. But it was no use. The voice still penetrated her mind.

'Mia... CANCAZANOTIA.' The voice in her mind spoke the word and a strange thing happened. Mia blinked her eyes open and let go of her ears. Strange, but somehow familiar memories flooded her mind, like a river that was out of control. Everything was happening too fast.

'No-no-no!' she repeated and fell back onto the bed. She closed her eyes and rolled from side-to-side. Her forehead glistened with perspiration, which pooled in her eyes and rolled onto the pillow. She was shaking violently and found it hard to breathe. 'Stop-stop-stop!' she shouted, and then, as soon as it all happened, it stopped. Mia lay still on the mattress. Her whole body was drenched in sweat. Her breathing calmed and the anxiety inside subsided. She sat up and saw the ghostly apparition of OBSIDIAN! He was literally floating in front of her eyes.

'But you were banished?' she stammered.

'Yes, that is true, but not any more. You must understand, Mia – you, too, are a wizard.' Obsidian said calmly.

'I am a *wizard*?' she said simply.

'Yes, my dear, you are,' Obsidian confirmed.

'H-how is that possible?' she pressed.

'I kept you safe by hypnotising you. I didn't want to, but I had to stop Jenta-Lor finding out that you are, in fact, a wizard too.'

'I don't know what's happening. I can't handle this,' she said.

'Just breathe and close your eyes,' Obsidian said softly.

'It's coming back. I am a wizard,' she said, and opened her eyes wide. 'I can feel the energy inside.'

'Do you believe me now?' the ancient warlock asked.

'Yes, yes I do,' Mia confirmed, as her face lifted into a broad smile.

'You have to take down the "damper field",' Obsidian continued.

'Damper field?' Mia said, and then it filled her mind. 'Yes, the damper field.' She nodded towards the apparition and she now knew what she had to do.

'You have powers, do you remember?' Obsidian said.

'Yes.' Mia smiled when she answered.

'Jenta-Lor will soon know you are a wizard and he will try and take you down before you break his spell. But I will try and distract him so that you can help us overpower him,' Obsidian instructed.

'But what about this damper field?' she said with concern. 'Won't my powers be muted?'

'We are attacking Jenta-Lor as I speak. He is already distracted and can't focus on you and our attack, so his magical powers are low – the perfect time to attack the field. You must enter the room where the spell is held and shut it down now!'

'I know where it is,' Mia agreed, thinking of the room she'd been forbidden to enter.

'I will help you,' Obsidian added, and his image dissolved. Mia wasted no more time and got dressed right away. As soon as she made her way to the door, she heard commotion outside the house and realised everything rested on her.

She grabbed the handle to her bedroom and turned it. The door opened and standing in the hallway was Morbid!

'Are you going somewhere?' he said, his beady eyes trained on her.

'Just going to get a glass of water,' Mia lied.

'I'm afraid you're not going anywhere,' he insisted and stepped into the room. He heaved his puny chest and smiled. Mia immediately stepped back as fear filled her whole body. Could she do this?

'You can't come in here without permission. Jenta-Lor will hear of this,' she argued, but knew it was futile to resist.

'It was Jenta-Lor that sent me,' he squeaked with a grin. 'Put out your hands.' She looked down and he was carrying a pair of handcuffs.

'What's happening outside?' Mia asked, as she tried to deviate from the conversation.

'That's none of your concern. Now, you must slip these on and come with me,' he said and reached out to grab her. But as he did, she felt something inside her that she hadn't felt for a very long time... the warmth of magic!

She smiled and didn't feel afraid any more.

'No, I won't,' she said with conviction, and Morbid looked puzzled. This wasn't supposed to happen. She looked confident and now he felt fear.

'I said you're coming with...' but he didn't finish what he was going to say. He was about to lunge at her, but suddenly felt taller. How was that possible? When he tried to work it out, he looked down and realised that he wasn't standing on the floor. He was, in fact, floating above the ground... suspended in mid-air! He dropped the handcuffs in shock.

'I-I,' but he couldn't get any words out. Mia, on the other hand, was enjoying every minute. But she also knew that the power she now held would only last so long. She needed to shut down that damper field. She realised that Jenta-Lor would soon know she was using power and he would be here soon.

She knew the ruler was preoccupied at the moment, but that wouldn't last long. As quickly as stamping on a rather unwelcome cockroach, Mia spun Morbid around until he was totally dizzy, and then tossed him across the room. He crashed against the wall, there was a groan, and then he fell to the ground with a dull thud. He didn't move after that. She could hear more loud noises from outside of the house and flashing lights cut through her curtains. She also heard footsteps closing in on her room. Jenta-Lor's police were going to arrest her; she had to escape right now and shut down that damn force field.

She quickly searched Morbid's body for a bunch of keys. She'd seen him carrying them many times and there was one room in particular that she wanted to investigate.

'Ah,' she said, as she dipped into his breast pocket. There they were. She took them and left her bedroom and made sure to shut and lock the door behind her. They would discover Morbid soon enough, but every little barrier was essential to give her precious time.

Mia knew where she had to go. She'd been imprisoned long enough to know what room was off-limits, and that was where Jenta-Lor's powers lay.

She could hear a full battle taking place outside and speedily swept along the corridors. She could feel new magical energy coursing through her whole being. How is this possible? she thought; it couldn't just be Obsidian boosting her powers, there must be others. She suddenly felt so powerful and realised that she could do anything.

Soon, police guards approached; they didn't stand a chance. She dispensed with them with the flick of a wrist. It felt so good to be in control.

Mia finally came to a stop at a set of double doors – this was it. She peered at the highly-glossed, wooden surface. She had the key to open it, but disregarded that thought. She concentrated her newfound powers and blasted such a force, the doors not only burst open but also splintered into a million pieces. Her magic was at full capacity so Jenta-Lor's powers were definitely weakened; now was the time to strike.

Mia stood as clouds of dust floated in the air. She squinted through the white fog and realised that the room wasn't empty! Inside stood a figure.

Unafraid, Mia stepped into the room. The guard stood firm, a formidable figure. She realised that Jenta-Lor wasn't going to let just anyone guard his secret. It wore armour of pure red, which covered it from the top of its head to its feet. On the front of the faceplate was a slit, which revealed pure white eyes. As if the appearance of its body wasn't enough to put fear into anyone's heart, it had a rapier gripped in its hands. Mia stood calm and not in the least bit intimidated. She felt she could do anything.

'Give up now and I'll spare you,' Mia spoke softly, her tone full of conviction. The creature didn't reply, but Mia didn't expect it to. All she needed was for it to relent, but deep in her heart she knew it wouldn't. As soon as she'd uttered the words, it advanced.

The guard raised its mighty sword, ready to cut her in half. It immediately sliced a diagonal line through the air with such force and speed, but Mia was wise to the attack and quickly side-stepped out of danger, making the guardian miss completely. But it didn't even appear to be off balance. Mia was shocked and quickly tried to plan her next strategy. Not perturbed by missing her, the creature immediately swung around and struck again. This time it was a lot closer, too close in fact. The sword came down fast and hard with no sound. Before Mia could get completely out of the way, it grazed the material on her sleeve and sliced through the cotton, taking a thin layer of her skin.

Mia winced as she leapt out of the way. Now was her chance! The creature was adjusting itself in order to make another move. For a split-second it was out of position. She concentrated her powers and sent an invisible force from her fingertips. It ripped straight into the mid-section of the creature's body. In that microsecond, Mia thought she heard it scream. Her magic had cut in deeply and soon a black, tar-like solution spewed out from the fresh, jagged wound. It spilled down the red surface of the armour, tarnishing it with black blood.

It tried to recover, but Mia could see the wound was causing a lot of pain. Hampered, but still determined, the monster once again lifted the sword in another manoeuvre. By the time it had lifted it halfway, Mia fired off another deadly blow. A violent surge of energy shot from her fingers and hit the intended target head on. It stabbed straight through the slit where she assumed its eyes were. There wasn't a screech this time but a full-blown, high-pitched S-C-R-E-A-M! Yellow fluid oozed from the open slot and ran down the face visor like amber snot. That was it; the creature was stopped in its tracks. It was just a statue.

Immediately, Mia felt weakness inside; her power was draining. She had to fight through that and stop the damper field. The wizard moved to the centre of the room where a plinth was set. On top of it was a glass dome and inside the dome, a swirling ocean of black liquid.

This dark mass seemed to sense that something powerful was about to approach. It sloshed back and forth inside the glass like a mini tidal wave. Mia had to crack open the globe and destroy the liquid right there.

'You have our combined strength, Mia… do it now!' Obsidian screamed inside her head. Mia let loose with everything she had and the room was immediately filled with a blinding light. Morbid stood outside and was about to enter with the handful of troops he had left, but thought better of it and left. The light got brighter and brighter and came to a peak. The glass dome, under so much pressure, began to crack like an egg and then exploded!

*****

All the wizards on the ship felt the release at the same time. Now it was time to disperse their own damper field; they didn't need it now – their powers were fully restored.

'Hey, everyone… look!' Rhidian shouted as he peered down at the palace grounds. Everyone made their way to the handrail and looked over. They could see helmets being removed right, left and centre.

'W-hat happened? Rhidian, where am I?' Rhidian turned and saw that Shana was sat on the deck, her face pale but her eyes alive again.

'Shana, you've been used by Jenta-Lor,' Rhidian said. 'Try not to move, you'll soon come round. I'll explain it all later.'

'I-I don't understand,' she said, staring at her uniform.

'We'll soon have you on the ground,' Rhidian said with reassurance. Alba walked over and gave her a bottle of water.

'Stay there, my dear. We still have things to do,' Alba insisted.

'He's lost his army now,' Caleb said with relish.

'But we still have to find him and secure him for good,' Obsidian added. 'Let's get down there.'

Chapter 34
The Rise of Ruin

All was against him and everyone thought that Jenta-Lor was about to give in. He was cornered. His so-called army of police soldiers were now out of their trances, the power he'd held over them lost. It seemed that there was no escape for the evil ruler.

The fog had totally dissolved and the sky was changing from night to day. The sun began to rise in the east, bringing warmth and light. So was it almost all over? All the wizards had to do now was to take control and lock up Jenta-Lor in Skytraz Prison, just like he'd done to countless others – including Red. But where was he?

The Horizon was settled on the ground and anchored in a field, far from the burning compound.

'Douse that fire, Red,' Obsidian called out, and Red targeted the burning drums and swept down from the sky and circled the compound. Shard blew an icy blast that cooled and smothered the flames, leaving clouds of white smoke. But the fire was finally out.

'Well done, boy,' Red said as he patted Shard's neck.

'My pleasure,' Shard replied with a grin, baring his huge pointed teeth.

'Where is he?' Rebus asked, the urgency in his voice grave. 'Jenta-Lor, where is he?'

'Trying to make his escape, I would have thought. I've a bad feeling though,' Obsidian revealed. 'Find Jenta-Lor and bring him to me,' Obsidian said to his wizard companions.

A terrible screech cut through the hiss of the diminishing fire. A shriek so loud that it hurt everyone's ears.

'Aaargh. That's painful,' Rhidian complained, trying to blot out the sound. 'What is that?'

Soon, from the clouds of billowing smoke, it came. Everyone looked in disbelief as a huge, black dragon took to the sky.

'What is going on?' Rebus gasped. 'Where did that thing come from?'

The dragon looked almost identical to Shard, except for the fact that he was black and not blue! It had the same long, narrow head, a beautifully curved neck and its torso was thick and strong, protected by a network of scales. The dragon's hind legs looked as though they could lift a mountain. Perched on its back was the person everyone was looking for – Jenta-Lor! The colossal, black dragon spread its vast wings to their fullest.

It was a formidable sight. Jenta-Lor then spoke and his voice boomed.

'You all thought I'd lie down and let you take over *my* city!' he bellowed, his eyes filled with hatred.

'It's not your city any more, Jenta-Lor!' Red barked back, as he and Shard flew towards them. 'Obsidian is in control once again.'

'Not if I can help it,' Jenta-Lor growled and moved in to attack.

'Be careful, Red.' Rhidian looked up from the ground, knowing full well that the boy couldn't hear him.

Red could feel Shard's body stiffen, ready to defend. Jenta-Lor's eyes widened and his grin turned into a wide sneer. They faced one another in the air.

'I'd like to introduce you to Ruin,' Jenta-Lor gloated, 'and that's exactly what he's going to do to you and your friends.' With that, the beast flew directly at them, the black dragon's mouth open wide.

Red had read the situation right away and knew the dragon was about to belch fire. So, too, did Shard. The blue dragon was wise to it too, and before Red could issue instructions, the dragon dive-bombed to the ground.

Ruin suddenly let rip with a stream of fire that burst from its throat. The yellow- orange flames lit a trail across the sky like a flaming spear. The people below scattered and ran for cover. The wizards themselves had to shade their eyes from the sheer brilliance of the firestorm.

Luckily, with Shard's quick thinking, the fire reached its peak and evaporated before it did any damage. While all this was going on, Shard had circled around the back of Ruin and blasted a stream of fire of his own. Jenta-Lor was no fool and easily guided his dragon out of harm's way. Shard gave chase, with Red willing him on. They were cunningly trying to push Jenta-Lor and Ruin from the bystanders and away from the city.

It was almost daylight now as the two dragons scorched across the morning sky. They looked magnificent. It was certainly an impressive but deadly show. Red knew that they were far enough away from Valusha to really battle one another without endangering innocent people. He also knew that he was a novice against Jenta-Lor – a seasoned wizard. But, being a dragon rider and a wizard was deep inside him now. He just had to let it out. He had been practising as much as was possible in the time they'd had together.

Shard was about to fire off another volley of flames, when Ruin, guided by Jenta-Lor, turned in double-quick time and swooped directly underneath the blue dragon's body. The two beasts collided and Red almost fell off Shard's back on impact.

Ruin stabbed his sharp horns deep into Shard's underside, which left two puncture holes. The blue dragon screamed with an ear-splitting shriek. He was left badly wounded and winded, so much so he lost control of flight.

Shard fell to earth at a rapid pace, gasping for air, blood pouring from the fresh injuries. Red hung on for dear life and shouted intensely at Shard to level off.

'Shard, Shard!' he ranted. 'Pull up, pull up.' The boy gasped, tears streaming from his eyes and taken away by the wind. But the dragon was still trying to breathe and continued to descend towards the sea. 'SHARD, you have to pull up!' Red screeched into his ear. That seemed to do the trick and the dragon came back to his senses. He was breathless and in pain, and moving at such a speed it was almost impossible to level off.

They could both see the shimmer of the blue surface fast approaching and Shard eased back his head. He came to within metres of the sea and pulled out of the dive. They went from a decline to horizontal and into an incline in a split-second, and ended up skimming the surface of the water. Foam and seawater splashed in Red's face and the salt burned Shard's wounds.

'If you wanted a dip you should have asked,' Red joked, and then he saw the blood dripping down Shard's legs. 'Shard, you're hurt.'

'I'll be fine,' Shard winced. 'We have to stop this right now, before it gets out of control.' Soon they were soaring back up into the blue expanse. But where had Jenta-Lor and Ruin gone? Then Red's newfound magical powers told him they were right behind! The boy wizard suddenly heard the crackle and hiss of Ruin's throat as it readied for another gush of flame.

'Faster, Shard, faster – lift, lift!' Red bellowed and gripped his horns as tight as he could.

'I-am-trying-Red,' Shard gasped, the pain obvious in his voice. Ruin let out a line of fire that caught the tip of Shard's tail. The blue dragon screamed and pulled away quickly at a different angle.

'Quickly, Shard,' Red said urgently. 'Turn around now and fire directly at Ruin's belly – the same as he did to us.' Shard realised what Red could see: Jenta-Lor was too preoccupied. He was looking back at the city, thinking that this battle was almost over and that was his mistake.

Red yanked at Shard's horns and pulled to the left. Shard was fully in position and urgently let loose a blast of wild fire that struck the black dragon's underside. By the time Jenta-Lor realised what had happened… it was too late.

Shard's concentrated flame cut a long gash along the underbelly of Ruin. The black dragon suddenly exploded into a colossal fireball which quickly dissolved into nothingness.

'I knew it. Ruin was just a spell. One of Jenta-Lor's party tricks,' Red gushed. Immediately they heard the screams of Jenta-Lor as he fell towards the sea.

'Should we rescue him, or let him drown?' Red asked.

'You can't let him die – he has to answer for all his misdeeds,' Shard said, and broke into a dive. They caught up with his falling body before he hit the cold water. Shard grasped him between his teeth and held fast.

'Let me go – let me go,' Jenta-Lor protested, but the dragon's jaw was too strong.

'You'll need my help to keep Jenta-Lor from breaking away.' Obsidian's voice seeped through Red's mind.

'Yes, master,' Red answered.

But as Jenta-Lor tried to break free, he suddenly found himself weak and as stiff as a starched shirt. 'You're not going anywhere,' Red expressed, as he felt the surge of magical energy pulse through his veins. He knew exactly what to do and how to do it, but it was with the help of Obsidian.

Red had combined his magical energy with the old master, and Jenta-Lor was trapped with invisible ice. He could only move his eyes, the rest of his limbs paralysed.

'Let's take him back to Obsidian, Shard. He'll know what to do with him,' Red added. 'Thank you, master, I know I have a lot to learn and, with your help, I can be a strong wizard some day.'

Red could see that Shard was in a lot of pain; they had to get back and repair his wounds. 'It isn't far, Shard. We can make it, my friend. We'll soon get you well again,' Red said, but wasn't sure at all if the dragon was going to survive. Shard flew as fast as he could back to Valusha.

Red felt his life had just changed forever – he was truly a wizard now and, hopefully, if Shard was well again, a dragon rider, too.

Chapter 35
Old Ruler Returned

Mia stepped out of the palace into the blazing sun and the first person she saw was her husband, Rhidian. His eyes were glistening and, so too, were hers. They ran towards each other and locked in a loving embrace.

'I'm so happy that you're all right,' Rhidian said, his voice muffled as he snuggled in her shoulder.

'Me, too. I've got something very important to tell you,' Mia said, but didn't have the chance, as Shard appeared and came in to land. The people were scared and backed away, but they soon calmed when they saw Jenta-Lor, the ruler they despised, locked in the mouth of the dragon.

'Please!' Red shrieked, his voice wracked with urgency, 'Shard is hurt.' Then the dragon swooped in, very unsteadily. He crash-landed and came to a stop on his side. Jenta-Lor fell from the dragon's open jaw and rolled over, but couldn't get up. There was a lot of murmuring in the crowd and the wizards came in to help.

'What happened?' Caleb said when he saw Shard's wounds.

'The black dragon dived straight for his belly,' Red sobbed.

'He's lost a lot of blood,' Alba conveyed with concern, as he surveyed the damage. Shard's blue eyes were watery and weak. He slowly began to close them and Red could see how serious the situation was.

'Don't go to sleep, Shard. Stay awake please,' Red cried. 'Someone, do something.' Mia broke through the crowd and with the help of the other wizards, linked hands and concentrated. Shard appeared very weak and took one last breath. 'No, don't you die, Shard. You must stay awake,' Red insisted, tears flowing onto Shard's cheek, but his head dropped to one side.

Soon, all the wizards held a yellow glow. The blue dragon closed his eyes and the power of the sorcerers began to take effect. The bloody gouges slowly closed and eventually, after a minute or so, Shard's belly looked healed again, but the dragon was near death. The glow of magic diminished and the wizards stepped back. There was no more they could do. Silence crushed the murmurs and all stood deathly still.

A huge weight of sadness consumed everyone. Obsidian looked at the crowd and the wizards, and was about to speak when Shard slowly opened his eyes. In the next seconds, wild cheers and laughter spread all around. Red hugged the dragon as tight as he could.

'What's all this fuss about?' Shard spoke, and the laughter lifted even higher.

It was now Obsidian's time to do something. He felt that he had to address the people. Rebus picked up on this and gestured for him to move inside the palace and onto the balcony.

'Good idea, old man,' Obsidian mused. 'This is a special time and I need to reassure these people that this won't ever happen again.' His eyes were focused and his mind grasped for what he had to say.

While Obsidian and Rebus disappeared into the foyer, Alba and Caleb noticed someone dressed in black trying to make his escape. The two wizards were about to stun him with magic, but a right hook from Rhidian sent him spinning.

'That's for what you did to me, Morbid, you weasel,' Rhidian grinned, satisfaction written all over his face.

Obsidian stood on the balcony, and amplified his voice so that all the people could hear what he had to say. The crowd hushed and looked up.

'From this day on, everyone is welcome in these gardens. Come and hear what I say,' Obsidian insisted. With that, the gates were opened wide and lots of people poured in. There was trepidation at the sight of a fully-grown dragon on the front lawn and Obsidian could sense that. 'Shard will not harm you. In fact,' Obsidian called out from on high, 'if it wasn't for his help, we would not have defeated Jenta-Lor.' There was a general coo from the crowd. Once the whispers and murmurings had subsided, the great wizard spoke again.

'I was forced out of office and exiled from Valusha by Jenta-Lor, as you all well know. He said he didn't want wizards and magic inside the walls of the city. You all agreed with him.' There was an uncomfortable ripple amongst the people. 'So every wizard was either exiled or imprisoned, but for what?' He shook his head in dismay and stood silent for a moment. 'What was life like under the rule of Jenta-Lor?' Obsidian asked. There was another pause and then someone from within the crowd spoke.

'Life was terrible,' a man said. 'He taxed us heavily and treated us like his personal servants.' The people agreed and a chorus of low groans erupted. 'Life was so much better under your rule, sir. This man tricked us into believing that *you* were the evil one,' the man relented. 'I think, looking around at everyone here, we are all truly sorry,' he apologised.

'Life can go back to the way it was,' Obsidian said with a warm smile. 'And the ironic thing is, Jenta-Lor himself,' and he pointed to the wizard when he spoke, 'is a wizard, too.' There was a chorus of booing that filled the air and then, as Obsidian raised his hand, the roars dulled.

'I want you to give me the same respect that you gave me before all this nonsense took place,' the old wizard said honestly. 'And when I finally retire, my granddaughter, Mia, will be the next in line to rule Valusha.' He pointed to her and she looked as stunned as Rhidian.

'*You* are Obsidian's granddaughter?' Rhidian said and he looked numb.

'The wizard bit, I was about to tell you – the granddaughter part, I didn't even know myself until now,' she spoke honestly. 'I am as shocked as you are, Rhidian. You have to believe me. It must have been that damper field. It took away the memory of nearly everything, except you,' she said. 'That's probably because inside the force field I didn't know I was a wizard,' she spoke honestly. 'I now realise that Obsidian is my grandfather and also that my parents died in a freak accident when I was a baby.' There were tears in her eyes and he hugged her again. Rhidian realised right then that even the wizards were kept in the dark by the damper field.

The surprise announcement was soon turned from gasps into wild cheers. Obsidian turned to Rebus.

'I realise now, master, why I couldn't remember that you had a granddaughter,' he puzzled.

'It was the force field, Rebus. It took away all the wizards' memories. But I knew there was a wizard inside the city, my intuition told me that. And now I know it's my granddaughter, Mia,' he said with relief.

Obsidian then turned to the people and raised his hand to quiet the crowd one more time. 'I now declare this day as a holiday. All taxes will be reduced to a more sensible level. And no one will be forced to join the police service any more. If you want to be a Valusha Police Service Officer, then job applications will be handed out. Magic will never be used for evil ever again in Valusha. Further more, Jenta-Lor will go directly to Skytraz Prison to serve out the rest of his days. And all innocent prisoners will be released immediately. I will be appointing new people into employment positions to help throughout the city – wizards and citizens are equal. Now… it's time to relax and enjoy our new holiday. Tomorrow the real work begins to get the city back on its feet. Thank you, citizens of Valusha.'

There were huge cheers for their old ruler, who was now their new ruler again. Rhidian and Mia welcomed Mia's grandfather, Obsidian, into their new family. There were a lot of tears but joyous ones. Rhidian was reinstated as the engineer. The couple returned to their home and lived a great life. It took a bit of getting used to, but

Rhidian finally accepted Mia as a wizard. The other wizards were welcomed back with open arms. And even Shard was pampered as he was Valusha's new mascot. Red became a fine wizard and once Shard was back to full strength, Red became a skilled dragon rider too.

Jenta-Lor was put into solitary confinement and is still there to this day. Morbid was exiled and hasn't been heard from since. Valusha is safe once more.